Praise for the 13 Reasons for Murder Series

"…hard to put down and am keen to read the next in the series."—Reader's Favorite 5-Star

"Full of sass, good friends, and a bit of blood, this novel was a joy to read."—Julie E.

"…suspenseful, addictive…hope there are more books with this character."—BookBub Review

"I look forward to…learning more about Britney."—Studiohnh.com Review

"…oddly addictive…cannot wait for the next book…"—Amazon.ca Review

"…flows at a quick pace and leaves you wanting more…" —Goodreads Review

"The plot is fresh and unique, a nice change to read something a little different…"—Reader's Favorite 4-Star

"…well written and kept me on the edge of my seat…"—Heather W.

13 Reasons for Murder: Betrayal

13 Reasons for Murder #6

Amanda Byrd

Blacksheep Press

Contents

About the
Author

Amanda has a love of horror and borderline obsession with fictional serial killers. She frequently makes *Hannibal*, *Harry Potter*, and *Dexter* references in "normal" conversation. She is also a full-time psychology major. When not writing, Amanda can be found reading, playing video games, or watching shows and movies like *Mindhunter*, *Hannibal*, *Harry Potter,* or *Dexter*. Amanda currently resides in Tampa, Florida with her husband and two cats.

Follow Amanda online: www.amandabyrd.net
Sign up for the monthly email list and get a free story

For my readers,
Thank you for sticking with me through the tough times. I appreciate you always.

One

THE SKY WAS ON fire. I tried not to get too lost in its beauty as Stu drove. The oranges and yellows and reds that could only signify the beginning of sunset in Florida. Pinks and blues would show the deeper down the sun fell. I couldn't think of a more beautiful way to celebrate Barb and Jim moving in together.

We came to a stop at a red light, and Stu looked over at me with love in his eyes.

"One day people will be celebrating us like this," he said, smiling. He took my hand and kissed it.

For the first time in a while, I was at a loss for words. I smiled back at him just before he turned his attention back to driving.

"I love you too," I finally replied.

Stu snickered. "Took you long enough."

I sighed. I was at some level of peace that prevented me from being my usual sarcastic self. In a dark corner of my brain, I heard a muffled scream. As though something were being held captive by that internal peace. I hoped that thought was wrong. At least for today. If it weren't, I'd have a lot of blood on my hands once it broke free. But would the blood be a problem? A smile lifted only the left corner of my mouth.

I continued to watch the sky as Stu drove. Before I knew it, we were pulling into the apartment complex Barb and Jim had moved into two weeks ago. The scattered palm trees at the entrance swayed lightly in the breeze. The buildings were painted with an odd combination of colors: light blues and bright red-oranges and pale yellows. The contrast reminded me of a child's coloring book.

We followed the signs to Barb's building number and parked a few spots away from her car. As I got out, I looked around. The sight of Julie's car made me smile.

"I don't even know who else was invited," I said, almost mumbling.

"Does that matter?" Stu asked. "It's not like we're staying too long, anyway."

I shrugged. "Nah. I guess I'm just not really up for a party with people I don't know."

Besides, I already have my next-to-die picked out. And that means I have plans to make.

We reached their door, and I pressed the button for the doorbell. The door swung open so fast, I had to wonder if someone had been standing there waiting.

Barb flashed a blinding smile. "You're here!" She wrapped me in a hug that I was pretty sure stopped my heart for a few seconds.

When I could breathe again, I congratulated her. "This is such a happy day for you. Congratulations!"

Stu hugged her after she set me free. I was still catching my breath as she returned his hug and let us in. Then I handed her the gift-wrapped box I was carrying. The look on her face admonished me for giving them a gift at all. I grinned back at her. She knew there was no stopping me.

Julie and Cody were talking to Jim and a couple other people I didn't know over at the breakfast bar. I nodded at them and kept looking around. The open floor plan made the place seem way bigger than I was positive it could have actually been. The foyer opened to a living room and dining area. The kitchen was off the left side of the living room.

Barb set the box on the dining table and rushed back to me, pulling Julie with her.

"Let me give you the tour," she squeaked.

Julie and I glanced at each other and nodded, smiling.

"I don't know about her"—I nodded to Julie—"but I expect nothing less."

Julie raised an eyebrow and smirked. "And here I was thinking Britney could be the tour guide," she said.

Barb giggled, grabbed our hands, and pulled. Stu, Cody, and Jim watched and waved as we were led out of the room.

She stopped us first in the middle of the living room. There was a sunroom that looked more like a small room extension off to the side. In it sat a few chairs and a coffee table. The view was of a wall or fence that was covered in ivy. It was serene enough to have a few cocktails there and chat the day away.

Then Barb led us through the dining area to a very short hallway, if it could even have been called that. On one side was the door to the bedroom. On the other, a door to the water heater closet. And directly in front of us was the door to the bathroom. Since it was right there, I walked in. It was a decent size for the two of them. There was even a linen closet, which was more than most apartments had.

The bedroom had a walk-in closet, typical of Florida living. Bedroom closets in other apartments, or states for that, left a lot to be desired. I know. I'd seen some of

them. The bedroom itself was a good size too. It almost equaled the size of the living room.

I arched an eyebrow and whistled. "This place is nice, Barb. Congratulations!"

"Yeah, it feels comfy here. Great location too," Julie chimed in.

I'd never seen Barb happier.

"Thanks ladies! I'm glad you like it," she said.

"You're the one who lives here," I said.

"Yeah, but it makes me happier knowing you like it. You have such good taste," Barb said. She was glowing so much, I was almost afraid she'd burst.

A group hug ensued, and when Barb pulled away, she was wiping tears from her cheeks.

"I'm just so grateful—" Her voice broke and she started crying.

Julie and I glanced at each other, not entirely sure how to handle happy tears, as we'd each only experienced them once that I knew of—and never over moving in with someone. Barb, however, was a sensitive person; that much was obvious. I went into the bathroom and plucked a tissue from the countertop, handing it to Barb when I walked back out.

She nodded her gratitude. "I'm sorry for all the tears. I'm just—"

"So happy?" I asked, smiling.

Barb nodded and giggled.

Julie took her hand and led us out to the living room. "It's cocktail time!"

Two

STU AND I STAYED for a few hours. Just long enough for me to nurse a single glass of wine. The sky was shrouded in the fog of streetlights when we walked out.

"Well, damn," I complained.

"What's up?" Stu asked, opening the car door for me.

"I was hoping the sky would still be purple when we left, is all," I said buckling my seatbelt.

"We can watch the sun set another night, babe. Tonight was about friends and celebrating their happiness," Stu said when he got in.

"Yeah. You're right." I sighed.

The peace I'd felt earlier was diminishing, and that little voice that had been held captive was growing louder.

Kill that bitch. You know she betrayed you. But first, get her to confess to the real reason she quit working for you. The patients hating her was a fucking lie. What's she hiding?

By the time we got back to my place, I was ready to start my planning and preparations for Becca. And that snobbish husband of hers, Bobby. This was as much about him as it was about her. I'd had a feeling he'd been the one who told her to betray my trust in the first place.

I wandered to my front door, lagging behind Stu, lost in thought.

Becca and I had been close. I'd loved her like family; she'd told me I was like family to her. Fuck that bitch.

So lost in though was I, that I hadn't realized Stu stopped to unlock the front door. I walked face-first into his strong back.

He turned around and looked at me, concerned. My face was twisted in anger and frustration.

"You okay?"

"Oh. Uh, yeah. I guess. Sorry, I was just thinking."

"Thinking pretty hard," he said, bending down to kiss my forehead. "Come on, let's go inside." He turned around and opened the door.

I was still foggy, trying to clear my mind of the anger at Becca. How could she call me family then fuck me over so hard? Who did that? Shitty people, that's who.

Without realizing it, I'd taken my shoes off and wandered into the kitchen. The cool of the open fridge door brought me out of my fog. I looked for wine but didn't find any.

"Shit," I said as I closed the door and turned around to face Stu.

"What's wrong?" he asked, smirking. He had a wine glass in his hand and a bottle in the other.

"Never mind," I said, a small grin on my face.

I sat down at the table and Stu brought me the full glass. It wasn't full like a restaurant would serve; it was my kind of full. The top of the red liquid stopped about a half inch from the rim of the glass. Then he took a beer from the fridge as I waited for him to join me before taking a sip.

Once he was seated, I reached my glass halfway across the table and nodded. Stu reached his beer bottle over and tapped my glass, nodding.

"You really are the best boyfriend. How did I get so incredibly lucky?"

Stu blushed. "You're cute. What else can I say?"

I snort-growled. "Seriously. You're breaking the oath you took as a cop. For me. What did I do that makes you feel so much for me? Am I secretly a witch and cast a spell on you? I don't get it." I gulped more than half my glass down. "What makes me so worth the risk to you? And don't tell me it's because you love me because that's fucking bullshit."

Stu sat there looking hurt and possibly offended. "Wow, Brit. We were having a really good night and this is where you wanna take it?"

"I'm a masochist in more ways than one." I shrugged.

I chugged the rest of the glass and went to refill it. The remainder of the bottle filled it and I twisted my wrist to give the bottle a dirty look. "This is why I spend so much on wine. Fucking small bottles are only good for two glasses."

I tossed the bottle into the recycle bin and stood there, drinking like it was juice. Technically it was grape juice, even if it was fermented.

Stu watched me silently. I stared at him, waiting for an answer.

"I know you're not drunk, but what's got you so worked up?" he asked.

"Don't answer my questions with questions," I retorted. "I'm sorry. I was just thinking about that cunt Becca and her snotty husband. It was obvious when we ran into her that we knew each other once…"

"It was," Stu agreed with a nod. "Is that what got you asking these questions?"

"No, I asked because I genuinely want to know. It's been bothering me to know that I somehow corrupted you so much." I sighed. "I'm supposed to be the one with no feelings. Instead, it seems that you are." My shoulders slumped as I finished the glass.

Stu came over to me and wrapped his arms around my waist.

"I've always known I had a dark side," he said, his eyes boring into mine. "I never really embraced it until you trusted me with your secret." He kissed my forehead.

I looked at him crossly, my face showing my puzzlement. I was at a loss for words, so I just sat there. Not quite in shock, but also shocked enough. His words were things I'd never even dreamed of hearing from him.

"How dark? Like you-would-kill-people-just-because dark? Or…"

He shook his head and took a swig of his beer. "Nah. I always felt like I lacked some level of empathy. I'm not saying I'm not empathetic at all, but it's less than what most people have. Does that make sense?"

"Of course it makes sense, bonehead. I'm a murderer."

Stu chewed his lip for a long moment, then sucked in a sharp breath before speaking again.

"When I was a kid, I watched something happen. Something no one should ever have to see. I think it made the once-sensitive person I was cold. And dark. I haven't been what most call normal since that day."

"I'm sorry, babe." I kissed his cheek.

He smiled. "Don't be."

We clinked our drinks and sat there in silence for a while. Stu's face didn't reveal what was going through his mind, like mine did most times. Mine showed consternation and usually annoyance.

I stood, cursing under my breath. "Fucking cunt."

Stu stood and placed a hand on my elbow.

"Hey," he said softly. "What can I do to help you stop thinking about her tonight?"

I turned to face him somberly.

"I honestly don't know. I…" I looked down at the floor for a few moments. Then I lifted my face to meet his gaze with a grin. "Wanna help me sharpen my knife?"

"You're a special kind of twisted, Britney Cage," Stu replied, his eyes sparkling. "I'd love to."

Three

I BROKE INTO A jog headed for my bedroom closet and the safe held within it. Once I got there, I punched the code in and eagerly pulled the door open. The light reflected off the textured black shelving inside. I smiled broadly, recalling some good times with the equipment lovingly placed on the shelves.

I pulled the knife case from its home on the middle shelf and opened the box. The Cerakote colors winked at me, and I caressed the blade then closed the lid. Setting the box on the floor next to me, I reached back inside the safe and pulled the sharpening kit out. I placed that next to the knife and took a mental inventory of the supplies I had at that moment.

There were a couple syringes and half a vial of ketamine left. *Note to self: Reach out to veterinarian friend and get more. Diabetic needles are cheap enough in quantity; pick those up too.* I also still had a roll of duct tape and more than enough contractor bags. The box of replacement blades for my box cutter was more than three quarters full.

I thought about going out to check the bag in the back of my Jeep, but knife sharpening came first. Then I could go pull the bag to see what it needed. As it stood, if there weren't any in that bag, I'd need to get nylon rope too.

I pushed the door closed only because I didn't want Minion getting in there. That cat was mischievous and curious enough that she'd hurt herself in there. And I didn't want to try to explain to my vet friend how my cat managed to shoot herself. The Glock was in a holster and the Smith was in a case until I could find the right purse to carry either one in. A pencil skirt didn't exactly lend itself to appendix carry and still be concealed.

As I stood, I plucked the knife and sharpening kit from the floor. I trotted happily downstairs and into the kitchen. Stu was at the table, drinking what I figured was a newly unopened beer while he waited for me.

He looked up when he heard footsteps walking toward him. Then he chuckled.

"Want a tissue to wipe your mouth? It looks like you've been drooling."

I shrugged and winked. "Wouldn't you like to know?"

I sat across from him and slid the knife box across the table. He grasped the box in one hand and lifted the lid with the other. I watched as a smile spread across his face when he reached in to take the knife from its resting place. He held it up and twisted it around to examine at it better.

"Cerakote," he said and nodded approvingly. "Buck knife…custom…six-inch blade…" He whistled. "You went all out. Now I understand the reason for the drool."

He set it on the table and smirked at me.

"You didn't test the blade," I said, leaning forward eagerly.

Stu picked the knife back up and ran it across the top of his forearm. Arm hairs fell onto the table like some weird kind of snow. He smiled lovingly at the knife before setting it on the table, an expression that I noticed.

"It could use a good sharpening," he said.

"It's kinda sexy that you want to help. I mean, I already find that sharpening it is an act of love. Even if it does turn me on a little. It's also calming."

Stu nodded, acknowledging the sensation. "Like cleaning a gun."

It was my turn to nod. "Agreed. Let's get to it so we can have our own sexy time afterward."

He grinned seductively then reached over and took the kit. Before even opening the stone arms, Stu skimmed the instruction book.

"I don't want you to kill me if I fuck up your knife," he said before he let out a nervous giggle.

"I wouldn't kill you. I'd make you pay for a new one though." I smirked.

"Fair enough," he said and got to work.

I watched him run the blade over one of the stones. This was the first time this knife had been sharpened with this kit. When I bought it, I'd taken it to a professional and asked for tips and his suggestion for beginner sharpening kits. This one hadn't been cost effective up-front, but it would save me more in the long run.

My eyes had glazed over, watching Stu's soft, competent hands work the blade with the stone. I was feeling incredibly calm by the time Stu finished. I smiled and took the offered blade in my hand. Then I did as he'd done earlier and caressed my arm with it. All of the blonde hairs I'd had were now on the table. I threw my head back and chuckled softly.

"Stewart Jones, we are soul mates," I said, gazing into his eyes.

"It would seem that way." He stood, folding the stones back into the piece they were mounted to, and kissed me. "What do you say we take this upstairs?"

I stood and placed the knife in its case. Then I closed the lid, clutched it to my chest, and started off. Stu followed, sharpening kit in hand. When we got to the safe, Stu's eyes lit up.

"You don't mess around," he said admiring the safe.

It was a top-of-the-line model that I'd paid a pretty penny for—with no regrets. One could never be too deliberate when it came to something like a safe. After all, it was something that usually held a person's most valued things. In my case it held guns, knives, and other tools I needed to kill people. Or defend myself.

"You'd be surprised how little I actually paid for it," I said, grinning.

Stu arched an eyebrow. "Really? From where?"

"I did some research and found the best deal for the money, plus easiest installation. Basically, I found this sucker online and I've never been happier with an online purchase in my life." I lovingly caressed the door as I closed it and pushed the button to lock it up.

Stu pulled me close and kissed me. When he pulled back, his eyes were glittering.

"Now, where were we?" he asked.

I leaned into him as far as I could and kissed him. We simultaneously made out and maneuvered to the bed where we disrobed before falling onto it.

After we were finished, we lay there, me staring at the ceiling, Stu staring at me. My body felt like a million fireworks had exploded inside simultaneously and was now limp from the fire.

I rolled to my side and fell asleep almost instantly.

Four

THE NEXT MORNING, I awoke to the feeling of being watched. When I opened my eyes, I found that I was.

Peering through a half-closed eyelid, I found the source.

"Why are you being a creeper and watching me sleep?"

Minion responded by head-butting my chin.

A small smile crossed my face as I petted her and rolled over. I managed to open both eyes to see that Stu wasn't in bed.

"Well. Fuck me then, I guess," I said to the air as much as Minion the cat.

I rolled back over and out of bed. As I did, I glanced at the alarm clock. It read 10:07. At least that helped me understand why I was alone in bed. I brushed my teeth and went downstairs.

The scent of fresh coffee filled my nostrils as I padded across the tile floor into the kitchen. Stu sat at the table staring out the patio doors. He must have heard me come in because he turned to look at me.

"Morning," he said and sipped his coffee.

"Morning."

I poured my coffee, added a few cubes of ice, and sat next to him.

"Whatcha lookin' at?"

He sipped before replying. "The ducks. They're so carefree and fun. Do you think they have complicated emotions like we do?"

I nearly dropped my mug. "Like humans or like you and me? Because we are much different than typical humans." I forced a chuckle. I was uncomfortable making that statement, though I didn't know why. I suspected it was because I still felt like I'd turned Stu into some kind of monster.

"Like you and me. Because we really are much different than typical humans." He still watched the ducks as he sipped.

"I think they have basic needs, and they show some form of affection, but that's about it."

We sat there in silence for a few minutes. I finished my mug and remembered I still had some bird seed left. Standing, I walked to the sink and as I placed my mug in it, I spoke.

"Come on, let's go feed them. I have plenty of seed in the garage."

"Cool. But I'm bringing coffee," Stu said.

"Ehhh, I don't know how wise that is. If you break my mug I may cry. Or you might if bird seed gets into your coffee."

Stu smirked. "You're absolutely right." Then he chuckled, and we walked upstairs to get dressed.

The weather was less than typical for this time of year, more humid but cooler. Normal January weather was cool-ish but not as humid as today. I hoped it would lessen throughout the day, but Florida likes damp and gross.

The ducks didn't seem to mind either. They quacked and squeaked happily as they waddled over to us. Stu laughed.

"Do this often?"

The ducks came right to me and stopped about a foot away. Their little tails wagged so hard that it made me wonder how much it would hurt if I got hit by one of them. Would it be like the abuse from an excited Labrador tail? I bent down, and as a group they backed up a few inches.

"It's okay," I said, trying to soothe them. "I won't hurt you. And neither will this guy." I jerked my head at Stu. "Are ya hungry?"

I tossed a handful of food toward them and they fought over it then ate. Then it was gone and they were begging for more. I looked at Stu and he nodded to the bench I'd sat on last time. We walked over, and Stu tossed some more to the ducks.

When we ran out of seed, the ducks minded so much that, again, they followed us to the corner of my patio before stopping.

"Yeah, you do this often," Stu said with a chuckle.

"It's actually only been once before. And they stopped right there last time, too."

"Really?"

"Yeah. Weird, right?"

"Yes."

"I suppose it's a good thing, too, though. The last thing I want is to fight with a neighbor about the ducks begging. Or worse, having to hear about duck shit on the sidewalk." I let out a mirthful giggle.

Once we were back inside, Stu went right for the remaining coffee.

"Want any?" he asked, his voice fading as he got farther away.

I started back to the kitchen. "Nah. Water and wine. Not together; that's gross. But I could use a glass of water. I think I'm a little dehydrated."

"More for me." Stu shrugged and sipped. "Ow!"

I laughed. "That's what you get."

Stu chuckled and gave me the finger.

"Love you too," I said. Then I turned to the pantry and pulled out a bottle of water.

"I've been meaning to ask you: Why do you keep that there? And why you keep the pitcher on the counter."

"Because room temperature water doesn't hurt my throat when I chug it. And it hydrates better." My tone was that of a know-it-all. "Sorry. That sounded bad."

"You're good," Stu said pouring the last of the coffee into his mug.

I downed the water and poured a glass of wine. Stu watched me, but not in a judgmental way. I was relieved that he didn't ask if it was too early to be drinking. I'd have had to break up with him for that kind of negativity.

I shuffled into the living room behind Stu and we sat on the couch to take in a prerecorded version of the day's weather forecast. As luck would have it, the humidity was supposed to hang on through the day. Also as luck would have it, we didn't have to leave the house the rest of the day.

I turned to Stu and an ironically twisted smirk crossed my face.

"Looks like naked, inside, with the air on high is the forecast for the day." My tone was rather flat.

"Don't sound so sad about it, Brit," he joked.

I poked him in the ribs, and we both giggled, unable to hear the rest of the forecast. We stopped just in time for the whole on-screen seven-day graphic.

I shuddered.

"Look at that. It won't be so oppressive the rest of the week. When we have to work." The sarcasm dripped like venom.

Stu chuckled. "You have to work all week. I'm off on Tuesday."

"Maybe I'll take Tuesday off then. If for no other reason than to annoy you all day." I followed with an exaggerated maniacal cackle. Stu laughed at me as he stood and walked back into the kitchen, mug in hand.

"Want more coffee?" he asked from the kitchen.

"Are you serving it?"

He emerged from the doorway with the carafe in one hand, his mug in the other. Then he set his mug on the coffee table before refilling mine. I blew him a kiss as he straightened up.

"I tip well." I smirked as I said that.

Stu just chuckled and kept walking. When he came back, he sat down, sipped his coffee, and pulled the remote from my hand.

"Hey!"

"That's what you get," he teased, then giggled.

I nodded sharply and smirked, leaning forward to pick my mug up and take a swig. Somehow, I resisted the urge to let Stu know that I didn't burn my mouth.

Stu flipped around the different apps I had installed and settled on Prime. Once inside that app, he navigated to the Shudder channel. An excited squeal broke from my throat and Stu turned to gawk at me. I was a horror geek. Plus, it counted as research.

"What the fuck was *that* about?"

I cleared my throat. "Nothing," I responded sheepishly.

Stu laughed. "Uh-uh, no way. You're not gonna wiggle out of that. Was there something you wanted to watch and didn't want to tell me?"

"What? No! I'd never let you just choose while I sat back in silent hope that you'd pick exactly what I wanted to watch."

Grinning, Stu shook his head at me.

"If I wanted to watch the Kane Hodder documentary, I'd tell you. I mean, I do want to watch it, but not right now. But there is a movie I put on my list a while ago. Can you look for it?"

Stu sighed. "What if I told you I wanted to watch *House of 1,000 Corpses?*"

I squealed again.

Stu rolled his eyes and pressed the play button.
Today was going to be a great day.

Five

BY THE TIME THE movie was over, I was giddier than when it started. Stu was, too. We looked at each other simultaneously and smiled, as if thinking the same thought.

I nodded and took off up the stairs. Stu followed at the same speed and we raced each other to change into jogging clothes.

"I know it's really nasty out there," I said, muffled by my shirt as I pulled it over my head. "But even sex won't burn all this energy off."

"As much as I agree with that statement, it sounds weird. Sex is always my first thought when I have this amount of energy," Stu replied.

"Oh? Were you a slut before we got together?" I grinned and chuckled.

"Hah!" Stu burst into a sarchotic cackle. "You've known me how long? Was I ever this attractive?" He rubbed his abs for dramatic flair.

I snorted in spite of myself. "Fair enough. You were absolutely not hot when we first met."

"Thanks for your support, babe," Stu said before donning another T-shirt.

"No problem," I said as I lost my balance and fell into my leggings.

I shrugged it off while Stu started laughed.

"You deserved that!"

"I did," I said with a grin. "I totally did."

Downstairs, Stu and I stretched. When we were done, we went out through the garage, using the keypad to close the door.

It took a bit to get across Bayshore, owing to the time of day. We usually jogged before seven a.m. It was a few minutes after noon.

We grinned at each other, again reading the other's mind, and took off in a race. The good thing about it being so late in my day was that there weren't many people on the sidewalk. That meant that we had minimal obstacles to dodge.

Three minutes later, we slowed to a stop, breathing hard. I stretched and so did Stu. We didn't say a word as we recovered from our labored breathing. I paced as I stretched my arms because I was never one to stand still for long. I caught Stu smiling at me as I turned to see if he was finished.

"What?" I asked.

He shook his head. "You're cute when you can't stand still. Is this a normal thing for you?"

"Yep. It's not an all-the-time-kind of thing. More like lots of the time. I've been tested for ADHD but don't have it. Doc says I'm 'normal,' whatever the hell that means. Is that even a real thing? Normal?"

Stu hugged me, and I instinctively cringed then shuddered. My skin crawled at how sticky we both were. I pulled away as I placed my hands on his chest and pushed.

"Okay, then. No more touching you today." Stu joked.

"After we shower," I said as I jogged back toward my street.

Stu followed, and we took it much slower than race speed. At times, we even dropped down to a brisk walk. We didn't talk much on the way back, either. I found myself lost in feeling gross and badly wanting a shower. I figured Stu was thinking the same thing.

As we walked back into my neighborhood, Stu spoke.

"I cannot wait to wash the sticky off of my skin. You were so right to push me off of you. I'm sorry. Can you forgive my mistake?"

"Of course I can. Now you know not to do it again because it doesn't gross just me out." I snickered as I punched in the code for the garage door.

We went inside and drained a whole pitcher of water before doing anything else. I even turned the air conditioning up to help us cool off enough to get out of our sweaty clothes. I didn't want a repeat of getting changed to go for the jog in the first place.

Stu refilled the pitcher and sat across the table from me. We admired each other; he took in all of my features as if for the first time, as I did his. He reached over intending to touch my face, but I pulled back. Stu held his hand up, a silent acknowledgment of *my bad* and went back to the pitcher. He brought me a full glass. I nodded and tipped it to him before taking one last deep swig.

The urge hit like a gut punch and I stood from my chair and half walked, half jogged to the guest bathroom.

"You make a great penguin!" Stu called after me.

When I got back into the kitchen, Stu wasn't there.

"Where'd you go, shithead?"

I heard a muffled, "up here." So I walked upstairs and found Stu washing his hands, and heard the toilet running. I snorted.

"Serves who right now?" I smirked.

Stu smiled back at me as I started the shower.

"No, you're not coming in with me," I told him as I undressed. "It'll get warm enough in there without you adding to it."

Stu sighed and pouted. "Fine. I'll wait here like a good boy then." He plopped onto the bed and turned the TV on.

I kissed his forehead and got in the shower. When I was finished, I didn't bother to turn the water off since Stu would be getting right in. He had anticipated when I'd be done and was waiting on the other side.

I was startled when I pulled the curtain to the side.

"Took you long enough," he said.

"Yeah, yeah. You know how accident prone I can be and yet here you are scaring me like that."

"I'm sorry. I didn't mean to scare you this time. Next time I'll let you know I'm out here." He grinned.

I stepped out and wrapped my hair in a towel, thinking about how far our relationship had come in such a short time. How being with Stu affected most parts of my kills. Sure, he didn't influence the who or how or why, and I hoped that he never would. My kills were just that. Mine. "Thank you." I kissed his cheek and started to dry off as he stepped in.

Stu squeaked when the water ran cold but stayed in for another minute. I was lying on the bed staring at the ceiling, happy to be calm for the first time in a few days. Stu came out, towel around his waist, and watched me before putting the same pair of basketball shorts that he'd slept in.

"Hey, Brit?"

"Hmm?"

"Mind if I start keeping clothes here? Having only one or two changes isn't enough anymore." He lay back on the bed next to me, looking at the ceiling.

I shrugged. "I don't see why not. Want to help me clear some space for you in the dresser? The closet? Both?" I asked almost absentmindedly.

Stu hesitated. "Whatever works, I guess."

"They're your clothes, you tell me what kind of space you need."

Stu rolled onto his side, looking at me. I rolled over and read the confusion on his face.

"What?"

"Well, I was expecting you to be a little more…you. Like I thought you'd fight me on it."

"Don't be silly. I knew this time would come and—honestly?—never really thought about how I'd react or what I'd say. Anyway, it only makes sense that you start keeping more clothes here since we're here most of the time. When was the last time we slept at your place?"

"Never," he said matter-of-factly.

"Oh."

"It's okay. I like it better here. Though I wonder why I'm still paying rent there since I'm hardly there anymore…"

I didn't say anything; I knew where he was going with that line.

"Brit?"

I closed my eyes. "Shh. I don't know if I'm ready for this conversation yet."

Stu nodded. "Okay." He stroked my face gently and I opened my eyes. He was smiling, like always.

"You sure smile a lot," I said.

"Because I'm happy when we're together."

I shoved him playfully. "You are so cheesy! We are the furthest thing from a Hallmark movie."

We shared a giggle before I rolled off the bed and rubbed my stomach. "I'm hungry. Are you?"

A devilish grin spread on Stu's face. I shook my head. He stood and advanced on me. I turned and jogged down the stairs.

"Sustenance, dammit," I said plopping down on the couch with a chuckle.

He plopped next to me after handing me my phone. "Fine. Thai? Burgers?"

"Burgers because grease is my favorite."

Six

AN HOUR LATER, WE were stuffed full of grease, cheese, fries, and burgers. I'd eaten two of them and an order and a half of fries. Stu had watched in horror as I plowed through both burgers.

"For a small person, you really can eat!"

I shrugged. "If I didn't jog all the time, I don't think I'd need the calories. Besides, you kicked my ass today. Of course I ate two burgers."

"I did win," he said grinning.

"Yeah, yeah. Don't be a dick about it." I grinned back and kissed him.

We sat back and flipped through the apps trying to figure out something to watch.

"If it wasn't so gross outside, I'd say let's go feed the ducks again, but I really don't want to have to wash my hair again," I said. "I want to do something other than watch TV."

Stu giggled like a twelve-year-old.

"Not that either. I love you—and we have great sex—but no."

"I know," he said. "I'm just immature at times." He winked at me.

We sat there silent for a handful of minutes, each of us thinking about what we could do. Stu's light bulb idea happened first.

"Want to go to the range?"

"Great idea!" I practically jumped up from the couch and ran up to grab my guns and their cases from the safe.

While I did that, Stu plucked his dirty clothes from the hamper. "Want me to take these home?"

"Why? So they can grow mold? Leave them. We can stop while we're out for fresh clothes, if you want," I said placing the Glock in its case.

"Perfect," Stu said.

I held both cases in one hand as I closed the safe. Stu cocked his head to the side like a dog.

"No practice rounds?"

"Nah. I'll get some at the range."

"Okay, Miss Money Bags," Stu commented.

"You hush. I haven't made buying more than self-defense rounds a priority. Which reminds me that I need to practice more often. And to invest in practice stock."

"You know I'm just messing with you, right?"

"I'm sure there's a price difference depending on which range we go to. As long as the price is fair, I'm not complaining."

"You wanna pick where we go?"

"No, you probably have the hook-up somewhere," I said smirking.

Stu chuckled and shook his head as we walked downstairs.

I grabbed my ID, carry permit, and debit card from my purse, then put them in Stu's pocket. I didn't have any pockets of my own and knew better than to use my bra to hold things.

Stu opened the passenger door for me and I fell trying to sit down, like always. He smirked as he closed the door. I grumbled and leaned over to open his door as much as I could for him. He sat down and turned the key in the ignition. The engine purred and the exhaust growled. I smiled in appreciation of fine machinery. It may not have been a Jeep, but it was still nice.

Traffic wasn't awful, but it was still weekend traffic. It took thirty minutes to get to Shooter's World just to find out they closed in an hour and change.

"Do we even bother?" I asked Stu.

"Yes. Even if we only get a half hour, it's better than the nothing you've been practicing."

"Not gonna let me live that one down, are you?" I asked getting out of the car.

"Maybe after you've gotten a membership somewhere and go more than once a year," Stu answered.

I sighed as I pulled both cases out. Stu made a clicking noise at me. The one that told me to choose only one since we didn't have much time. I chose the Glock simply because I knew I'd anticipate the recoil, and the caliber alone meant more recoil.

I'd been in this place more than a few times, but never to use the range. It was all the way at the back, and there was a lot of eye candy distracting me. The distractions turned out to be a good thing because I still needed practice rounds.

"Babe, I need ammo," I said as Stu headed straight back.

"Oh, yeah," he said. "Make it quick. No other shopping."

"But Daaad," I whined.

He giggled. "Go. Quick."

"Not gonna help?"

Stu sighed and walked—dragged—me to one specific row. He had a brand preference and knew the store well. He picked up two fifty-round boxes and handed them to me.

"That's all you need for now," he said.

"But don't I need to have some at home, too?"

He picked up two more, then gently pushed me to the cash register. I pulled my cards out of his pocket, paid, and we headed back to the range area.

I didn't have safety glasses or ear protection with me, so I had to rent them, which grossed me out. Instead, I ran and bought another set of earmuffs and glasses. I was fairly certain I had both at home. If not, I'd have a new set regardless.

I jogged back after paying. Stu was waiting for me, targets in hand. I squeaked and jumped a few inches off the ground in excitement. The clerk behind the rental counter chuckled and shook his head.

I spun to face him.

"You hush. It's been a while, is all." I winked and grinned at him before turning back and following Stu.

"We have half an hour. Don't screw around, okay."

"Yes, Dad." I joked. "What's got your panties in a twist?"

"Nothing." He shook his head. "That came out all wrong. I'm sorry."

Stu opened the door and motioned for me to walk in first. I looked to him for direction on lane number and he jerked his head at number three. I nodded and continued on my way.

When I reached number three, I placed the case on the shelf and opened it. I noticed both magazines were loaded and frowned.

"Dammit," I grumbled.

"What's wrong?" Stu asked from behind me.

"Loaded mags," I responded dully as I pushed each round out and placed them all back in the case. "Guess I'll need more."

"You're hopeless," he said with a chuckle and a head shake.

"This trip was spontaneous. Besides, one can never have too many spare mags," I said matter-of-factly.

Stu smiled. "Sounds like I'm having an effect on you."

I opened one of the boxes and loaded both magazines with the practice rounds. I'd been so out of practice with just doing that, that I tore my thumb up in the process. Stu noticed and made a "tsk, tsk" sound. I rolled my eyes and slid one into place.

Stu had been busy placing a target and setting its distance while I was making myself bleed. I just needed to put on my protective gear and get to work. Stu donned earmuffs and safety glasses as he stepped back and leaned against the wall to watch.

"You're not shooting?" I asked him.

"Clear your mags first, and we'll see. Thirty minutes isn't much time."

I shrugged and got into position.

I got of three rounds before growling in frustration. I'd done precisely what I thought I'd do—anticipated the recoil. But the smell of spent brass and gunpowder lifted my mood, rendering it near-impossible for me to stay mad. I shifted on my feet, aimed, and concentrated.

Then I squeezed the trigger. This time felt much smoother. I kept going until the slide locked open. I dropped the empty magazine and clicked the full on in place.

When I was finished, I placed the weapon down on the shelf. Stu came back into the stall and pushed the button to bring the target to us. I guffawed at how torn up it was.

"Wow! That was some bad shooting in the beginning," I said. "But I definitely improved—"

"When you stopped anticipating the recoil," Stu finished. "You're actually a pretty good shot for not practicing."

I grinned. "Some people would call that being a natural."

Stu shook his head and chuckled. "Or that." He looked at his watch. "Mind if I run a full mag?"

"I'll even load it for you," I said eagerly. "I could use the practice."

Stu and I switched places, and he got into position as I leaned against the back wall.

A minute later, Stu had emptied the mag and dropped it from the gun. I'd have been lying if I said I wasn't impressed.

I walked over as he was bringing his target up. Mostly center-mass hits, with a few to the throat.

"And people say *I* have anger issues," I joked. "Seriously, how often do you practice?"

"Once a month, maybe," Stu said, shrugging. He threw the target in the trash and swept up as I packed my things.

Once I was back in the car, I could do nothing else but sniff my hands. There was something about that smell that relaxed me. It made me wonder what unignited gunpowder smelled like.

Seven

I DIDN'T IMMEDIATELY WANT to wash my hands when we got to Stu's apartment, but I did anyway. Probably because Stu wouldn't let me touch anything until I had. He didn't want it getting anywhere since he was never here to clean. I understood that.

"That reminds me…We have to clean my house. Or I do. But I feel like, since you practically live there with me…"

"Of course I'll help. I actually like dusting. It's so satisfying to literally watch something go from gray to clean," he said packing a bag.

"Who the hell are you? What kind of weirdo *likes* dusting?"

Stu snickered. "I'm your weirdo, lady."

That got a chuckle out of me.

Stu zipped up his bag and flung it over his shoulder. "Ready when you are."

I nodded and led the way out of his apartment and back to his car.

We arrived back at my house in record time. It turned out that Stu didn't live very far at all.

"Now I know how you always got here so fast," I said getting out.

"You mean when I wasn't already outside."

"Yeah. What the fuck, man? Why did you do ever do that?"

"I wanted to keep you safe after the incident with Sweet. Some of the others wanted to come scare you. I wasn't about to let that happen. So I'd sit here like a guard of sorts." He shrugged as he opened the front door.

I didn't know what to say, so I just smiled and walked inside.

Stu went upstairs while I headed for the kitchen.

"You coming?" he asked.

"Yeah, gotta feed the cat first."

"Okay," he said, his voice fading as we both got farther away from each other.

A few minutes later, I walked into my bedroom to see him ogling my safe. I couldn't suppress a giggle.

Stu spun around, his face pink, and lips tight. I grinned at him, signaling that there was no reason to be embarrassed. His shoulders dropped and he deflated like a balloon.

"So, where do you want me to put my stuff?"

"Up to you. Dresser? Closet? Both?"

"I'm not playing that game. You house, your choice," he shot back. "I don't want you mad at me on some random day just because you let me choose."

I sighed. "Ugh, fine. Dresser it is."

I walked over and emptied two drawers onto the bed. I didn't dump them but carefully picked up and placed the folded clothes there. Stu laughed at me.

"Mess with my OCD, and see what happens, buddy," I threatened playfully.

He held his hands up in a defensive pose and giggled.

"Okay, those two are yours," I said pointing to the open drawers.

"Damn, thanks," Stu said in a bit of shock. "I wasn't expecting that much space."

"Careful," I warned, "might be all you ever get."

"Ha!" Stu set his bag on the bed and began taking things out and refolding the pieces that hadn't stayed put in transit.

I pulled hangers from the closet and placed them into the clothes I'd pulled from the dresser. We'd both finished putting things away in under ten minutes.

Stu's stomach audibly grumbled. I snickered.

"Any ideas?" he asked.

"All you," I said. "For once, I'm not in a mood for anything specific."

The grin that spread across Stu's face made me momentarily regret saying that. I shook my head and walked down the stairs, Stu trailing behind.

I dropped onto the couch, and Stu pulled his phone out. I thought he was looking up dinner, but he started giggling.

"Food is funny?" I sat forward and pressed the button to get to the apps on the streaming stick.

"One of the guys sent me this meme," he said, putting his phone in my face.

It was the one about the NSA being the only ones who actually listen to Americans. I snorted and continued flipping through to find a serial killer documentary to watch. Stu noticed.

"Research?"

"Nah, just interesting. If I can learn something from it, that's just a bonus."

I selected one that I'd forgotten even existed, let alone was on my list to watch. I pressed the play button, then paused it so we could order dinner.

Stu looked up at me from his phone with a confused expression.

"Dinner?" I asked and stated at the same time.

"Right," Stu said and went back to paying attention to his phone and nothing else.

Some time later—I hadn't been keeping track, as I was interested in the documentary—Stu spoke again.

"Dumbass," he said.

I turned to face him. "Who are you talking to?"

He motioned to the TV. "Him. He's a fucking moron. How did he think he wouldn't get caught?"

"You make it sound obvious. You seem to forget that most serial killers are driven by control issues and a sexual element..."

Stu's head snapped in my direction. "Not at all like you. Why is that?"

I shrugged. "Because women are different? Because we're not driven by sexual impulse? Look at Wuornos. She was driven by a childhood of abuse.

It might not have been vigilantism, but she felt it was justified. Then you have Fisher. She fed men poisoned tea, and her husband stabbed them to make sure they were dead. Why? Because they wanted the man's money. And those were just a couple serial killers in the US who didn't fit your generalization." I crossed my arms over my chest and harrumphed.

Stu watched me, his face falling. "I'm sorry. I didn't mean to upset you."

"You didn't upset me, but you did annoy me with that generalization. And what did you decide for dinner?" I asked, changing the subject before I actually did get mad.

Stu shrugged. "Pizza and cheese sticks." He slid closer on the couch. "Babe, I am sorry. I didn't think…"

I kissed him lightly. "I know you didn't. Please think next time you're about to say some dumb shit." I grinned, kissed him again, then scrolled back to watch what we'd just missed.

Around twenty minutes later, the doorbell rang. Stu stood to answer it. I moved to pick up the remote, but Stu held a hand up.

"It's fine. This guy just pisses me off anyway," he said unlocking the door.

I stopped it and went into the kitchen for plates and napkins. Then thought better of it and only grabbed napkins.

Back in the living room, Stu glanced at me from the corner of his eye.

"What?"

A small smile creased his cheeks. "Nothing."

I heaved a sigh. "You're full of it," I said with a smirk.

"I am. Let's eat," he said sitting down. "Wait. Did you turn that documentary off?"

"Yeah. It's not like I can't watch it when you go back to afternoon or night shift. Besides, he was pissing me off too."

"Fair point," he said freeing the first slice of pizza from the whole.

Similarly, I pulled the first slice of cheese sticks from its whole. The gooeyness made me happy; cheese was my favorite food and I believed it should have been its own food group, outside of and apart from the dairy category. I bit into it and enjoyed the flavor of the three cheeses before putting something else on for us to watch.

Stu found something first. He tittered and mumbled something about being "cute when having a mouthgasm."

I finished chewing and swallowed. "Huh?" Cheese hung from the corner of my mouth and I slurped it up like pasta.

Stu chuckled. "I said you're cute when you're having a mouthgasm."

"Am I cute when I slurp, too?" I joked.

Stu shook his head and finished the slice of pizza in his hand. He handed me one as soon as I put the last bit of cheese stick in my mouth. I could only nod in thanks, for fear I might choke.

By the time Stu had finished his second slice, I had finished my first. I offered to break him off a couple cheese sticks, but he waved me off.

"Fine," I said like a child who had been told no. "I'll just take them on my next stalking adventure."

Eight

STU STOPPED PULLING A third piece of pizza from the box and arched an eyebrow at me.

"Take them *where*?" he asked.

I shrugged as I ate the pizza. "I know it's a bit out of my usual routine, but I'm gonna start stalking earlier in the process with this one. Sure, I killed the sisters, but they were together all the time. I've got Becca *and* Bobby to kill this time. Just because they're married doesn't mean they spend all of their time together."

"True. So when do we start?"

I shook my head. "Maybe I shouldn't have told you…"

"You can tell me you don't want me to go with you. It's not a big deal," Stu said. "Actually, it's probably better if you do it while I'm at work. This way, if a neighbor or someone calls you in, I can either give you a heads-up or be the responding officer."

"That's sweet. And brilliant. Should we swap vehicles those nights too? I mean, I hate falling into your car and the struggle to get out, but…" I held my hands up. "What do you think?"

"Does she know your Jeep?"

I shook my head. I'd had it for a few years, but it had taken all of that time to get it looking the way I wanted it to. As far as I could remember, it was still stock when Becca fucked me over.

"I say take it and see what happens. It's not like you haven't followed people in it before," Stu said taking another bite of his pizza.

I nodded and bit into another slice, thinking about what Stu had said. By the time I was finished, my mind was made up.

"Okay, I'll take the Jeep, and if something happens, we can swap. Sound good?"

Stu grinned at me, pepperoni stuck on his front teeth on purpose. "Soundth perfethct."

Playfully, I shoved him and laughed. Then panicked that I may have made him choke. I looked over at him to see him chuckling and licking his teeth. My shoulders slumped a bit in relaxation. Stu caught the movement.

"No, you didn't choke me," he said. "You know, you baffle me. Here you are, a fairly empathetic killer. And you fall in love with me and actually care if you kill me. You have friends you'd do anything for. And here I am, with only slightly more empathy than you. Friends I'd do anything for. And I'm in love with you. What does that make us?"

"A fucked up Bonnie and Clyde?" I half offered, half asked. "I got nothin' else," I shrugged.

Stu chuckled. "Better than nothing, I guess."

By the time we finished the pizza, it was just about 9 p.m. I yawned and Stu did too. We looked at each other and nodded, knowing the other was asking if we should go to sleep. It had been a wonderful weekend, and tomorrow brought work for both of us. My day would start earlier, but Stu's would always be more strenuous.

I fell asleep that night with dreams of my next catch.

Mondays were my favorite, and I rolled out of bed with a smile. Stu rolled to his side and watched me walk to the bathroom through half-open eyes. I got ready for a jog, but Stu stopped me.

He was looking at his phone and read me the current weather.

"It's raining," he said.

"Of course it is," I said. "But that doesn't mean I can't—"

Thunder sounded, interrupting me. And the sunlight that shone around the blinds disappeared. Then there was a flash of lightning.

"Or I'm not," I lamented. "Maybe I need a treadmill." To a degree, I was joking. I didn't need to jog every day, but I liked to. It helped me stay fit.

"We could go to the gym," Stu suggested.

I shook my head. "And I'd be late to the office if we did. It's okay. You can make breakfast though." I giggled.

Stu smiled. "I love the way you ask," he said pulling the covers off and putting shorts on. "Anything special?"

"Waffles, please. I'll make the coffee."

Downstairs, Stu mixed the batter, and I scooped the coffee. Ten minutes later, we were both sipping liquid energy and munching on buttery waffles.

"These are really good," I said not caring that my mouth was half-full, "What's in them?"

"Wouldn't you like to know?" he teased, arching an eyebrow.

"Keep your secrets, then. I won't tell you the secret to the best couscous you've ever had," I said.

Stu smirked. "Ha, ha, you're a comedian."

"I thought it was funny," I said before finishing my breakfast. Then I took my plate to the sink and glanced at the clock on the oven. "I have to get ready. Thanks for making breakfast, babe." I kissed his forehead as I walked upstairs.

Stu was on the couch watching the morning news when I came back down. We kissed goodbye, and as I left, I said what I always do. "I love you. Be safe."

Traffic, as usual, sucked, but I made it to the office by 9 a.m. I preferred to be a few minutes early, especially on Mondays. Barb was already inside, like always.

The door chimed when I walked in.

"Good morning, Ms. Cage!" Barb called from the kitchen.

"Morning, Barb!" I called back. "How was the rest of your weekend?"

Barb emerged from the hallway bearing two cups of coffee and handed one to me. I nodded my thanks and walked carefully into my office. Barb followed.

"It was nice. Thanks again for coming. And thank you so much for the espresso machine," she said. "You really didn't have to do that."

"I know," I said getting settled and sitting down. "But I wanted to. And I'm hoping you'll tell me how you like it—or not—once you've used it. When I picked it up, I thought about getting one for myself."

Barb grinned. "Jim loves it! He's used it four times already."

"You've had it for two days," I said, a little shocked.

"I know, but Jim adores espresso and is super—"

The phone on my desk interrupted her. I answered it.

"Passing Through—"

"Britney! I can't thank you enough for the espresso maker," Jim gushed.

I chuckled. "Did you hear us? We were literally just talking about your love for espresso."

Jim giggled awkwardly. "Well, I, uh…"

"You're welcome, Jim, truly. I'm glad you're enjoying it so much."

"I'll make you a shot next time you come over," he said. "Well, that's all I wanted to say. So, thanks again, Brit. Have a good day."

"Thanks. You too. Talk soon."

"Bye," he said and terminated the call.

Barb blushed as our eyes met.

I chuckled, then cleared my throat.

"Have you had a chance to check messages yet?" I asked her.

"I have. Nothing important. Just people calling in their availability," she replied.

I nodded. "Thanks. That means all of the important stuff is in emails," I said.

Barb nodded her agreement and dutifully walked out and got to work. I heard the clacking of the keyboard as I booted up.

Ten minutes later, I was neck deep in my inbox. Clients needing to renew contracts, clients needing more temps for their busy seasons…It was a day that would go quickly. That was why I loved Mondays. The speed at which the day went by rivaled a race car. The other days of the week didn't move so fast. Tuesdays were the polar opposite, no matter how busy I'd get. But today was still Monday, and it was over before I knew it.

"Hey," Barb said peeking her head in, "It's five."

I looked up from my computer. "It is?" I glanced at the clock in the corner of the screen. It read 5:02 p.m. "Shit. Cool, I just have to finish this email, and I'm done. You don't have to wait for me."

"You sure?" she asked.

"Absolutely. Go home. Have a good night," I said with a smile.

"You too, Brit." She turned and walked out, the door chiming as she left.

I finished typing my email, and as I clicked the send button, the door chimed again.

"Barb, really, you don't need to wait for me," I said.

"No, but I want to," he said.

Nine

I LOOKED UP AT the sound of the voice, and my face lit up like a star in the night sky. I leaped from my desk and smothered him in a hug.

"Joe! What are you doing here?"

He choked out a few noises as he pulled my arms looser.

"Oh god! I'm so sorry!" I pulled away and shuffled back a few inches.

Joe caught his breath. "I wanted to surprise you. And I haven't heard from you. I needed to know you're all right."

My face flushed and grew warm. I dropped my head and looked at the floor. "I'm sorry," I said. "I know you worry about me. I don't want you to worry."

"You're forgiven, Britney. And I will always worry. I love you; you're family."

"I love you too, Joe. I am sorry. I should have called. Or at least texted. Do you want to have dinner tonight? Stu's at work until 9 or so. I can cook something."

Joe smiled at me. "Let's go somewhere. My treat."

"Sure," I smiled back. "Let me lock up and we'll leave."

"Okay. I'll be in my car," he said.

I nodded and he left. I felt like something was wrong and he didn't want to tell me here, where I could freak out. I was paranoid; he'd had a heart attack and wasn't exactly taking care of himself. Marsha, his helper, sure tried. But Joe was a stubborn old man and set in his ways. If he wanted a medium-rare steak every night for a week, he would have one. He didn't care that it wasn't good for him. He felt that life was meant to enjoy because we only got one. While I agreed with the sentiment, I didn't want to lose him, either.

I grabbed my things and locked up. Joe rolled the passenger window down.

"Get in," he said.

"If it's okay with you, I'd like to take my Jeep," I said.

"Sure. Follow me."

I got into the driver's seat and started her up. I was about to shift into gear when Joe called.

"Where are we going?" he asked.

"Shit! Um, anything that's not pizza or burgers,' I said trying to think of somewhere casual. "Cheesecake Factory? Mexican? What about Outback or Cheddar's?"

"Outback sounds good," Joe replied.

"Cool. I'll call now and get us on the wait list."

"See you there," Joe said before his taillights faded then brightened when he stopped at the red light.

I called as I pulled out of my parking space and gave the host both of our names. By the time the call ended, I was already at the main intersection of Waters and Anderson, behind Joe. It didn't matter which roads we took; it was rush hour and would take forty-five minutes to get there either way.

Somehow, we made it in thirty. Thank my stars for small traffic miracles. Joe and I parked a row apart, but close enough to see each other getting out of our vehicles. Joe waited for me since he was closer to the building.

"I gave them both of our names," I told him as we walked to the door. "I wasn't sure if we'd get here at the same time and wanted to make sure we got a table."

Joe opened the door for me and we were greeted by a huddle of people near the host desk. I shot Joe a look of irritation, and he nodded, then walked to the host desk. He talked to the host for a few seconds before looking over at me and jerking his head in a *come on* motion.

I followed the host to our table, Joe behind me. We thanked the girl as we sat. I looked around at how busy the place was.

"I forgot how crowded it gets here around this time," I said.

"Everywhere is busy at this time of night," Joe said. "Even if we'd gone somewhere like Bern's, it would be crowded."

"Fair point," I said as the server walked up.

We both ordered water. I also ordered a Blue Moon without the orange garnish and Joe ordered a Bud Light. The server nodded and said he'd be back with our drinks in a few minutes. I eyed Joe suspiciously.

"Beer? You?" I was incredulous.

He smirked. "Well you are, so I thought I would."

A half-smile crossed my mouth. "If you say so. Is everything okay?"

"Of course. Is it wrong that I wanted to spend time with just you? It's been so long since you and I have had dinner, just us."

"It has," I conceded. "I hadn't realized it bothered you so much."

The server brought our waters and asked if we wanted appetizers. Joe ordered the mac 'n' cheese bites for us to share.

"Excellent choice," he said. "And I'll be right back with your beers."

We thanked him and got back to our conversation.

'Everything is fine," Joe said, not missing a beat.

I shook my head. "I don't believe you, but okay. How's Marsha?"

"She's well. She likes you. Thinks you're intimidating, but she likes you."

"I haven't said or done anything to her for her to feel that way," I said, confused.

"I know. I think it's how you carry yourself."

"Interesting," I said, taking a sip of water as the server set our beers on paper coasters.

We ordered our entrées and he left again. Immediately after, someone brought the appetizer to the table. We thanked them and I dug in.

Joe and I had a relaxing time together. The stress lifted simply by having someone else serve you—not at your own house—was incredible. We talked about his employees, and he asked how mine were doing. Specifically, Julie because he knew her well. He had yet to get to know Barb.

"When will I meet her, anyway?" he asked.

I swallowed my last bite. "Didn't you meet her tonight?"

His look was of disapproval. "That's not what I meant."

I hung my head. "I honestly don't know. Are you having a party anytime soon? I'm not planning one. And I think a dinner invite would be too intimidating. I think she'd feel pressured to join us and that it would make it more of a formal thing instead of casual for her."

Joe nodded in acknowledgment. "I get that. She's only ever talked to me in a professional way. She seems timid, which is weird for someone to be your assistant."

I spat water. "Shit, Joe. Make me seem like the scariest boss ever. But she's warming up. Stu and I were just at her and Jim's new apartment this past weekend."

"Is she less timid at home?" Joe asked. "I'm not trying to be a jerk. I'm sorry. I shouldn't have asked. She's your assistant, and if you're not all that close with her, there's no reason for me to need to get to know her."

I shrugged and waved for the server who was walking away from another table. When he arrived, I asked him to split the bill, ignoring that earlier, Joe had offered to pay.

"Nonsense! I'll take the bill, please," Joe said to the kid. The kid went kind of pale, nodded, and scurried away.

I scoffed. "You scared the shit out of that kid, but *I'm* the intimidating one?"

Joe chuckled. "I didn't mean to, honest."

When the server came back with the bill, Joe apologized. The kid graciously accepted it and the folio back after Joe slid eighty dollars inside.

"Keep the change," Joe told him.

This time, the kid's face turned beet red. He stuttered a "Thank you" and ran off.

"Thanks, Joe. I didn't realize how much I needed a night like this with you," I said.

We left and hugged at Joe's car.

"I really am sorry for that line of questioning about Barb. I guess I was just hoping you may have made a new friend."

I giggled. "I've got plenty of friends. And Stu," I added. "But I do like Barb. Maybe when she comes out of her shell more, I'll introduce her to the girls. She's definitely no Julie, though. That girl...Well, I adore her. But if Barb never comes out of her shell, I'll respect that too."

"Mixing business and personal lives is always a gamble," Joe remarked.

"You got that right," I agreed.

We hugged again and said goodbye. Joe got into his dark blue BMW and waved as he backed out. I watched him turn out onto Dale Mabry before getting into my Jeep.

As I pulled onto Dale Mabry a few minutes later, my phone rang.

"Hello?" I hadn't paid attention to the called ID because I was too busy paying attention to driving.

"Miss Cage? Miss Britney Cage?"

"This is she."

"This is Officer Smith from Tampa Police."

Ten

SHAE'S CASE HAD BEEN solved months ago. They'd arrested Michael, and he was in prison for the next fifty years or something. I couldn't figure out why this woman was calling me now.

"Yes. What can I do for you?"

"I understand you knew Andrew York."

"Knew? Has something happened?"

"I'm sorry, Miss Cage. I thought you were aware."

"Aware of what?" My acting was getting back to what it used to be. As far as I could tell, she had no idea I was playing dumb and concerned.

"He's been missing for a while. A classmate he was friendly with told us you'd placed him with one of your clients."

"I did. I placed him with an accounting firm as a junior accountant."

"That wouldn't have been James Accounting, would it?"

"Yes. That's it. His direct supervisor's name is Jim. I do remember Jim telling me that Andrew quit, but

I never heard anything from Andrew himself. Do you think something bad happened to him?"

"I'm just looking into the possibility. In truth, I think he just took off. He's the type to do that. And the classmate says Andrew has done it before."

"Oh, wow. I had no idea. Before we ran into each other, we hadn't talked since shortly after we graduated," I told her. It was mostly truth.

I backed into my garage and cut the engine.

"Was there anything else you needed, Officer Smith?"

"No, thanks. Nothing else for now."

"Okay then."

"Sorry to bother you. Have a good night. Oh! If you think of anything, please call me." She hung up without waiting for me to wish her well with this case.

I sneered as I dropped from the driver's seat. It was smart that she didn't expect to find him because she never would. The sea life had probably digested him by now. His bones were likely so far away and separated, there could be no hope of finding all of him.

I went inside and changed into something more comfortable for sitting in the Jeep for a few hours. I pulled a pair of Stu's basketball shorts from the dresser, along with a t-shirt. Then I tied my sneakers and grabbed the cheese sticks before heading back into the garage. I pulled a bottle of water from the back and hopped in.

I'd been to the Martin house many times. But that was a long time ago. I hoped they still lived there. The drive took around forty minutes, since most traffic was still headed north and so was I.

I turned onto Livingston and then onto Regal Oaks. A few houses down on the right, if I remembered correctly. And I did; they still had the same mini-van they'd had back then. And Bobby drove a Toyota sedan, which was weird given how he was snobbish about how much money he made.

My mind kept going back to the classmate that Andrew still talked to. It was possible that they were concerned about Andrew's disappearance. Or maybe they simply wanted to make sure that he was gone. I hoped it was the latter, but there was no way to be sure without knowing who the classmate was. Was it even someone I knew? Did they know me? I decided to keep an extra eye on my six until I could talk to Stu.

I shook my head fiercely, forcing myself to be present in the moment. I had parked a few houses down on the opposite side of the street from the Martin house. Streetlights were on, but the closest was blocked by an oak tree. The next closest was two houses away. I had a good view, though I'd be lucky to get one this good again.

Lights were on inside, and I saw a shadow move past the front doorway. It was one of those screen-and-glass storm doors and the front door itself stood open. The figure walked to the storm door, affording me a clear view. It was Bobby. He was on the phone and looked frustrated about something. I sneered and kept watching.

Less than an hour later, Becca came to the door and looked out. I saw her hand fiddle with something before she turned away and closed the front door. She must have locked the storm door. Tonight wasn't the night I'd try to find out, though. That would have to wait. Tonight was more for me to start planning my KKD.

I already had the kill planned. The disposal was a little less so. After all, I hadn't bought a kill knife for no reason. The disposal options were things I'd done before and knew beyond all doubt I could pull any of them off again. I only had to decide on one. It would come to me by the time I knocked them both out. Which only reminded me to check how much ketamine I had left. Syringes I still had plenty of.

I started the engine and drove off. It was 9 p.m., and Stu would be home soon. Besides, these two seemed to do nothing after an hour ago. A pang of jealousy hit me. Why was I jealous, even in the least bit? I had no reason to be. Stu and I had grown so close in such a short amount of time. But I still couldn't understand it. What could I *possibly* have had to be jealous over?

Money wasn't the answer, either. I'd had enough of that to live comfortably.

I took Bruce B. Downs to Fletcher and made a right. Again, I'd had multiple routes home, and none were faster than the other. The drive took between thirty and forty minutes.

When I pulled onto my street, I noticed a black on black Charger behind me. I grinned and took my time backing into the garage. The Charger pulled in as I shut the Jeep off and got out.

"Hey, babe! How was work?" I asked, walking toward him as he opened the rear door.

"Dull. You?" He threw his bag over his shoulder and kissed my forehead.

"Joe surprised me at the office, and we went out to dinner."

"Is that where you're coming from?"

"No. I was just watching Becca and Bobby and their boring Monday night," I said taking the empty cheese stick box out and trashing it.

Inside, Minion screamed as we entered the kitchen.

"Oh, hush. I fed you already." I scowled as I petted her. She nuzzled me and I picked her up.

Stu chuckled and petted her. "You're so spoiled, little girl."

"She is my child," I said as I set her back down.

Stu started to say something but stopped.

"What?" I inquired.

"Nothing," he said. "I'm pretty sure we're on the same page where children are involved."

I stopped at the bottom of the stairs, turning and eying him funny.

"Have you been planning a future with me?"

He cleared his throat. "What if I have? Would you complain?"

I turned and walked up the stairs, leaving his question hang for a moment.

"No, I wouldn't. Though I have to admit I haven't gotten all that far into our future yet," I said reaching the top.

"That's fine," Stu said. "I don't mind doing all the planning." He flashed me that adorable cheesy grin.

"I don't want kids," I said abruptly.

"Me either. That's why I said we were on the same page," Stu said, undressing.

I started the shower water for him and flung his towel over the shower rod. "Brian is a cool kid. And one I don't have to worry so much about. I'll stick with being an aunt."

Stu stepped into the shower and I changed into my pajamas. While I waited for him to finish, I went back downstairs to make sure the house was locked up. I crawled under the covers as Stu was shutting the water off.

"Wanna watch a movie or just go to sleep?" I asked.

"Movie," he replied without stopping to think. "One of the *Halloween* movies. But not the third one. That one was a serious fucking disaster that had nothing to do with anything."

I clucked. "*This* is why we're together!"

When Stu joined me in bed, I pressed the play button on the newest *Halloween*.

Eleven

Stu was in the kitchen pouring us both coffee when I walked in, yawning and stretching. I took the offered mug and thanked him in a mumble. Sipping it cleared the fog from my brain enough to tell Stu what I'd forgotten to last night.

"Officer Smith called me," I said sitting at the table.

"Oh?" He sipped his coffee then joined me.

"Yeah. She's looking into Andrew's disappearance. Some classmate apparently called and reported him missing."

"Did she tell you who the classmate is?"

I shook my head and drained my mug. Stu held a hand up for me to stay seated, and he retrieved the carafe. I tried to take it and refill myself, but he did that for me too. I nodded at him as he sat back down.

"No," I blew on it before sipping. "She did say that he's gone MIA before, though. She even made it sound like she didn't care; that she was just doing her job."

Stu nodded. "She probably doesn't care. Andrew, was a sleaze and I'm sure the classmate made that known." He sipped his coffee. "To be sure, I'll look it up when I get in. I'm sure we have no reason to be concerned."

I arched an eyebrow. "No? This is the second time she's come calling for someone I disposed of.

"You're fine. I've got you, now, remember? I'll do what I have to if it means you're safe." His eyes sparkled at me.

"I love you too," I said.

After we finished our coffee, I went upstairs to get ready for the slowest day of the week. Tuesdays were my nemesis days, as I called them, and I abhorred them. But they had to be lived, just like any other day. I closed my eyes and told myself I'd be all right, and that Stu would handle anything that came up, that the day would move fast.

I opened my eyes and sighed. I was lying to myself now. I would be all right and Stu would handle anything that came up. But the day would not move fast. Of that I was certain. I finished getting ready and kissed Stu on my way out the door.

At the office, my face didn't hide my dismay.

"What's wrong?" Barb asked.

"Huh? Oh, nothing. It's Tuesday, is all. You know how most people hate Mondays? I hate Tuesdays." I grumbled on my way back to my office.

"Oh," Barb said as she sat down at her desk.

Nothing more was said that didn't have to be for the next hour. I ruminated in my misery, and even that grew darker when I looked at the clock and saw that it was only 10 a.m. I grumbled to myself and went to the kitchen for some coffee. Halfway there, I changed my mind and pulled cash from my purse before opening the door.

"Going for coffee. Want anything?" I asked Barb.

She shook her head and I left.

I came back with a coffee for her anyway. She was grateful.

"You really didn't have to," she said, taking it from my hand.

"I know. But it's nice to change it up sometimes." I winked at her and went back to my desk feeling better. It was amazing how much a simple change of coffee flavor can uplift a sour mood.

Stu called at lunch, shortly after he clocked in for his shift.

"I checked the report. Turns out your pal Andrew had some issues. He was into a bookie for thousands. And that classmate? Her name is Lucinda Veil. She mentioned that Andrew has dropped off the earth before to get away from the bookie's thugs. She also mentioned that she wouldn't be surprised if he was dead. Something about him not taking no for an answer." He snickered.

"Well, then. I guess you were right."

"Seeing how Smith's already noted that she doubts he'll turn up anytime soon, yeah. You're fine."

I let out a relieved sigh.

"Good stuff," I said. "I'm glad she doesn't think I had anything to do with him going missing."

We talked a few more minutes before hanging up so both of us could to get back to work. A glance at the clock told me we hadn't been on the phone as long as I thought. At least my day was half-over.

I contemplated going to watch Becca and Bobby again tonight, but decided against it. I didn't want to chance one of the neighbors seeing me two nights in a row. Not this early in my stalking game, anyway.

After lunch, the day somehow managed to move even slower. Most days slowed down post-lunch, but today was fucking awful. It was like watching a sloth race.

Finally, five o'clock came and I found myself so excited that I leaped from my chair and did a happy dance. Most people reserved such things for Fridays. Not me. Tuesday was the real weekly stumbling block as far as I was concerned.

Barb and I each went home as soon as I'd locked the door.

"Bye," she said, waving as she dropped into her Honda.

I waved back and climbed into my Jeep. The night air was less than ideal, but it was a welcome change from the frigid air of the air-conditioned office. I even rolled the window down on the drive, though I did turn the air on, too, since the steam outside was thick enough to coat the inside of the windshield in a fog.

When I got home, I showered and fed Minion. Then I called Stu. I got his voicemail.

I left a message asking him if he'd eaten yet and for him to call when he could. I hit the end button and sent a text message saying the same thing. Thinking he may have eaten or that he could be busy the rest of his shift, I went to the pantry for a back-up dinner.

When I opened the pantry, I went right for the pasta. But I realized that by the time I would eat, it could be a little too late for that kind of sugar spike. So I went to the fridge instead and pulled out a package of grilled chicken strips and salad mix.

As I set the ingredients on the counter, my phone chimed.

Hey, babe. Already ate. See you soon.

"Ugh," I groaned and sighed.

Okay. Love you.

I set the phone back down after tapping send and got to work assembling my dinner. It looked appetizing and pretty when I was finished. The only dressing in the fridge was saesar, which was perfect, though I was missing the parmesan cheese. I shrugged and added the dressing and took a bite.

"Mmmm."

Minion looked at me funny.

"It's good. Don't judge me."

I finished the salad while standing at the counter. There hadn't really been a reason to sit down or go into the living room since I knew it wouldn't take long to eat. Setting the fork and plate into the sink, I mumbled about how much of a snack rather than dinner that had been. But I wasn't going to eat anything else because I hadn't jogged in days and I worked hard to not eat within a few hours of going to bed.

I flopped onto the couch after washing the dishes and flipped around one of the streaming apps mindlessly. I pressed play on *Dexter* for the familiarity.

At one point, he was injecting someone with M99, and it hit me that I wasn't entirely sure how much ketamine I had left. So I tore up the stairs and opened the safe. The bottle was a tiny bit above half-full. That meant I had just enough to knock both Becca and Bobby out. But I'd need more after this.

When I got back downstairs, I sent a message to my nurse friend asking for more. He responded that he'd send it out tomorrow. I thanked him and sat back, playing the show until Stu stomped through the door.

Twelve

Up the stairs and into the bedroom he went without saying a word. I almost would have felt insulted, but I also knew better. Stu didn't act that way unless he'd had a terrible night. I went up after him.

When I reached the top, I heard the shower water running. So I sat on the bed and waited for him to finish.

He came out wearing nothing but a towel around his waist.

"Wanna talk about it?" I asked.

"Actually…yeah. I do," he said pulling a pair of shorts from the dresser. Simultaneously, he pulled them on as he dropped his towel. Then he sat next to me on the bed.

For the next thirty minutes, Stu vented about how tough a day he'd had after hanging up with me. I reached over and held his hand as he talked. His face ran the gamut of emotions: from frustration to annoyance to sadness. Such was the life of a cop. He finished by telling me about the car stop that found him calling child services. The mother was so high that she barely had any idea that she had a child in the back seat. I didn't feel bad for this type of person, though I knew how tough addiction was to break.

I shrugged. "I hope she cleans herself up for good," I said as I hugged him.

"Me too," he said into my neck. "I always feel like shit when I have to call for a kid to be taken from their parent. Even when that parent is a junkie who doesn't even realize they have a kid at all."

Stu wriggled across the bed and lay down. I joined him and we fell asleep.

The nightmare I'd had before about being home and asleep when Sweet had broken in returned. I awoke to find myself screaming and covered in sweat. Stu sat up and was gently trying to wake me.

"What was that about?"

"It was the same nightmare I had a few months ago about Sweet…I was asleep when he broke in…" I wiped my face on my shirt. "I'm gonna go shower," I said and rolled out of bed.

Stu followed me into the bathroom. "What do you think it means?"

"I don't know. Maybe that I'm afraid he'll come back when he gets out?" I sighed as I flung my towel over the rod and stepped in.

I let the lukewarm water fall over my body like a waterfall. It was refreshing when it washed over my face. It felt like the thoughts ran down my body and into the drain. I hoped the nightmare wouldn't come true. Also that it wouldn't come back.

I wrapped the towel around myself after shutting the water off. Stu was waiting on the bed for me like I had for him. He patted next to him, and I sat as he wrapped me in his arms.

"We'll know when he's being released and can get a restraining order against him. Though I'm pretty sure a condition of his probation will be to stay away from you."

"I'm sure you're right," I said. "But we know well enough that those orders don't always have an effect."

Stu sighed. His face was wrinkled with concern.

"What?" I asked.

"I'm just worried about you," he said.

I hung my towel to dry and cupped his face in my hands. "You don't need to do that. But I love you for it." I kissed his cheek and we walked back to bed.

Stu lay down as I dressed into clean pajamas. Then he patted his chest, indicating that he wanted me to use him as a pillow. I happily obliged, and before we knew it, we were both out cold.

We awoke to my alarm, which was on the other side of the bed. I groaned and rolled over to shut it off. Stu rolled over and draped an arm around me. I wanted to stay in bed another half hour but was also still angry about the recurrence of the nightmare. I shifted Stu's arm off of me and rolled out of bed.

Stu moaned. "Ugh, really? Come back to bed."

"Still kinda angry about that nightmare. Come jog with me."

Stu moaned again, this time in jest, and got out of bed. We were ready to go in no time.

The weather was on the border of comfortable but beginning to feel humid. Overall, it was more tolerable than most of the year. We jogged our loop and zigzagged back to the house.

It felt good to pound the anger out on pavement. My whole body vibrated with the endorphin rush and a little bit of soreness, but that soreness made me feel that much better. Maybe I was a little masochistic in that sense, too.

Back inside, Stu had a brilliant idea.

"What if you work from home today?" he asked with an arched brow.

"I could…" I said. "Or I could just take the day off. It's not like I have a whole lot to handle that Barb can't manage on her own."

Stu's eyes sparkled mischievously.

"Okay." I nodded. "I'll call and leave her a message now." And I did just that before taking a shower.

When I went back downstairs, Stu was at the kitchen table waiting for me. There was a mug full of fresh coffee sitting in my spot, calling my name. I pulled a few ice cubes from the freezer and gently slid them in before taking my first sip. I groaned in pleasure.

"You make a mean cup of coffee," I complimented Stu.

"Thanks. Yours isn't so bad either," he said with a wink.

I sat down, and we didn't speak for what felt like a long time. We simply sat there enjoying our coffee and each other's presence. Stu watched me as I sipped my coffee and it creeped me out a little.

I set my mug down and went to get the pot—we both needed a refill. As I poured more, I side-eyed Stu.

"What?"

"You're creepy, that's what," I said then chuckled.

"How so?"

"You've just been watching me like a weirdo." I sat down.

Stu sipped. "Well, fine. I won't look at you anymore." He turned to face the wall.

I giggled. "Ass."

Stu smiled. "So what do you want to do today?"

"That's your department. You're the one who wanted me to stay home."

"Fair enough," he said and put his deep-thinking face on. It looked like he was constipated, and I couldn't suppress a laugh.

"What's so funny?"

"Your face," I replied between giggles.

"Why?" Stu was getting a little upset, his voice dipped then raised half an octave at the end of the question.

I straightened. "Because you were in such deep thought, you looked constipated." I sipped my coffee.

Stu blushed a little. "Oh," he said before burying half of his face in the coffee mug.

I thought for a few minutes, and an idea popped into my head. "How about we go to the zoo?"

Stu perked up. "I like that idea. We can make a day of it or something. It's been so long since I was there last."

"Me too," I said. "But, seriously, fuck the llamas."

Stu spat coffee on me. "What?"

Thirteen

Stu couldn't say anything. He was too busy choking on the coffee that had slid down the wrong pipe. This made me giggle.

"Serves you right for abusing the coffee that way."

When Stu was able to breathe without coughing, his face was still bright red, but he spoke.

"Why do you hate llamas?" he asked. Then he started giggling almost uncontrollably again.

I frowned and furrowed my brow. "You don't deserve to know now," I huffed.

I finished my coffee and set the mug in the sink, still faking upset.

Stu walked over and wrapped his arms around me after setting his mug in the sink, too.

"I'm sorry," he cooed.

I burst into giggle fits. "I was kidding about being upset," I said as I turned around to face him.

He frowned. "Oh."

"Was my acting that good?"

"Well…yeah."

I smiled in pride. "That's really good to know. For a while there, I was losing the ability. Glad it's finally back."

Stu's eyes inquired about the llamas.

"Oh right. The llamas. The first time I went into the petting zoo, those fuckers watched me. Just sat there like creepers and watched me. There were plenty of other people for those bastards to watch, but they chose me."

Stu cackled. "Let me get this straight. You hate llamas because they were creepy?"

I nodded. "Yes. And they're dicks. The only ones I like are cartoons." I was like an adamant child when I said that last bit.

Stu's face screwed up in confusion.

"I'll show you later. One of them eats people. It's great. Let's get ready to have a good day," I said taking off for the stairs.

By lunchtime, we'd traversed the Asia and Florida areas. I opened my map and eyed it, looking for the next part to walk around. Stu reached over my shoulder and pointed to the main aviary. I shook my head.

"We've already been through that one." I pointed to the lorikeet aviary. "We walked right by this one, though. I always do that. Dammit."

Stu shrugged. "Okay."

We spent about twenty minutes at the lorikeet exhibit. If we'd felt like paying the extra fee, we'd have gone in for a feeding experience. I still wanted to, so we asked about doing one after we'd eaten something. They said there was one around 2 p.m. We got our tickets and went to eat and have beers at the beer garden over by the meerkats.

I'd never experienced the beer garden here before, only walked by and looked at it. It was a cute area with a tiki-style bar. We ordered food and beers at an exorbitant price, and sat and ate. By the time we were finished, it was time to make our appointment time for feeding the lorikeets. I practically jumped from my seat in excitement. I bounced on the balls of my feet while I waited impatiently for Stu to get up.

"You're like a child. Do you know that?" he said rising.

"Yes. Yes, I absolutely do. Now, come on," I bade, pulling the rest of the trash from his hands and tossing it. Then I grabbed his hand and pulled him along. Reluctantly, he sped up without me expending too much more energy.

When we arrived at the lorikeet house, we were the only people in line to feed them. I looked at Stu, hope in my eyes—hope that we'd be the only ones inside, with the exception of any employees. Fortune smiled upon me then, and the handler/docent person who took us in mentioned that we'd been the only ones to buy tickets for that time block. I squealed in pure joy.

Inside the aviary, at least one of the lorikeets sounded like they were mimicking me. But then I realized that it was just their chirp. Dozens of them chirping at the same time. It would be tolerable for the short amount of time we'd be in there. Anything more than that would feel like being trapped in there with a handful of parakeets, eventually tortured by their incessant squabble.

Noise aside, I was ecstatic to be having the experience at all. I finally had a partner in crime—literally—to have such adventures with. None of the girls really had time alone to do geeky things with me and Brian wasn't as into being at the zoo as me. At least I knew I could go to Busch Gardens and Universal and the mouse park with Brian. Which made me wonder about Stu.

"Babe? Do you do amusement parks?" I asked as I petted one of the smaller lorikeets sitting on me.

"Random," he said. "But yes. Why?"

"Because I love them and now I can go with another adult," I said.

"Whose kid did you take?"

I looked at him, my face having zero chill, and he flushed, feeling stupid. "Brian."

"Yeah, but he doesn't always go on the same roller coasters as me," I said.

Stu nodded. "We can talk about that later." He smirked and nudged me.

While I was busy not paying attention, the small lorikeet had waddled its way up my arm onto my bicep and was watching me intently. Feeling apprehensive yet excited, I turned my head as slow as I could. We ended up virtually nose to beak. I smiled at it, and I swear it smiled back. It didn't matter that smiling was physically impossible for a bird. It bounced and chirped what I assumed was happily. The keeper giggled.

"He likes you," she said.

"Well, I like him too," I said bringing my other hand up in an attempt to scratch his tiny head. "Can I?" I asked the keeper.

She nodded and smiled.

I let the bird sniff my hand before trying to get closer. I'd never been bitten by a bird and didn't want today to be that day. I imagined it hurt like hell. He let me rub the top of his head and even nuzzled the side of his face against my fingers. Stu took a couple pictures so I'd always be able to remember this moment of absolute delight. The bird nuzzled my cheek again and seemed to almost coo. I resisted the urge to squeak again.

Our time in the aviary was nearing an end, and the hander plucked the small bird from my arm. I waved goodbye with my index finger—bending and straightening it almost like a worm standing up. Then I turned and walked out through the gift shop.

I was lost on a cloud somewhere when Stu's voice broke through.

"Brit. Hello? Britney?"

I shook my head. "Huh? Did you say something?" I was still on a high from the encounter.

"Yeah. I asked where you want to go next," he said grinning. He pulled the map out and opened it so we could both see it.

"Oh! Uh, back to Africa so we can watch the meerkats for a bit then hit Wallaroo on the way out?"

"Sounds good to me," he said, taking my hand after putting the map away.

At the meerkat habitat, I mentioned wanting one as a pet if circumstances—and laws—allowed. Stu just laughed at me.

Then we went to the area they called Wallaroo, which was also home to the petting zoo. Closing time was close at hand too; the zoo was only open until 5. But there was no line at the petting zoo, and I wanted to hang with the goats for a few minutes before leaving.

We entered, and the attendant explained the rules to us, making it a point to tell us not to go near the llamas.

Stu being Stu, he asked why.

"They spit and bite," the kid replied unamused.

I playfully pushed Stu into the sandy area and thanked the kid for not thinking Stu was funny.

"I told you," I said with a giggle.

Stu made a face at me and squatted down to pet an old black-and-white goat. He was promptly met with horns on his arm. I laughed.

"That goat always does that, and I don't know why."

"Oh, so you're used to this?"

"Yep! He's not trying to hurt you. I think he's trying to guide your hand or maybe when people pet him, he gets itchy." I held my hands up in a shrug.

About twenty minutes of goat petting passed before the attendant announced that the zoo was closing in another twenty minutes. Stu and I nodded at each other, acknowledging that we were ready to go.

We thanked the attendant, washed our hands at the washing station, and headed out.

Fourteen

WE STOPPED FOR TAKE-OUT on the way home. Burgers and wings and fries and mozzarella sticks were what I was suddenly craving. Stu was, too, so it wasn't much of a discussion. We went to that bar in SoHo that I usually went to for wings or burgers, and the wait was worth it.

Once we were home, it was difficult to not dig in before feeding a screaming Minion. She smelled the goats on me, too, and she was *pissed*.

"It's not like I brought one home," I told her.

Stu petted her head. "But she wanted to."

I shoved lightly him and he chuckled. "Don't worry. I won't let you. Now can we please eat? The smell is making me salivate."

I grabbed some paper towels and set them on the table. Stu pulled a few beers from the fridge and set them in our places after opening them. We sat and enjoyed our food without words for a while. Then Stu smiled and nodded at me.

"Good choice," he said, mouth full of chicken wing.

"Thanks for agreeing so quick," I said.

We clinked bottles and enjoyed the rest of our food in silence. Until Stu asked about Becca.

"So," he started before sipping his beer before continuing, "when will you head back out to watch her?"

"Ugh," I groaned. "Soon. Why? Want to join me or something?"

He shook his head. "I'd like to make sure I'm working in case someone calls on me."

"I've never had that problem before." I sipped my beer. "But it's been a concern plenty of times. Thanks. I appreciate it. I'll make sure you're working all of the nights I watch or follow them. Do you want to be there when I knock them out and take them? Or…" It was still weird to be discussing such things with Stu. I shifted uncomfortably in my chair and chugged the remainder of my beer. I stood and grabbed myself another, motioning to Stu to ask if he wanted another. He nodded.

I came back to the table and took the tops off before handing his over. He watched me, taking in my discomfort about our current subject of conversation.

"It'll get easier to talk to me about this, I promise."

"Will it though? You're a *cop*…"

"I know. And it is weird for me too."

My face twisted in disbelief, as if it took on the ability to say the words "full of shit" all by itself. Stu chuckled.

"I just don't get how you're so comfortable talking about this."

Stu shrugged. "I don't either. So I don't question it."

I eyed him as he drank his beer, the thoughts that I'd corrupted him running rampant in my mind. It was still possible that I'd made him darker than he already was; I wasn't ruling that out.

Neither of us said anything for a long moment. That moment, for me, was tense. I couldn't tell how Stu felt, though he looked relaxed. I mentally packed the conversation away and stood to clean the table. Stu helped, and when we were finished, we sat out on the patio. The weather was nice enough for it. We didn't sit out there long, however. I grew restless and needed something other than the darkness to occupy my mind.

Back inside, Stu pulled me close.

"You okay?"

I nodded. "Yeah. I just need…something. I'm not sure what. Maybe mindless movies…"

He led me to the couch and put on some B-horror. It proved to be exactly what I needed to get out of my own mind. The movie he'd chosen actually turned out to be one of the better zombie movies I'd seen in a long time. I grabbed my phone and looked it up. I grinned when I saw the news that there was going to be a second one. Then I told Stu, who reacted the same way.

It was still early-ish, but we both had to be in early tomorrow; Stu's shift went back to days.

"Bed?" I asked.

Stu sighed after looking at his phone for the time. "Yeah, I guess. I need to get used to going to sleep earlier anyway." He stood and helped me up. I checked the locks while he turned the lights out.

We lay in bed, and I stared at the ceiling, fighting to go to sleep. I wasn't tired. I was anxious. Stu was simply awake. I rolled over and turned the TV on to something that would hopefully make us both fall asleep. Stu laughed when he saw what it was.

"Really? The hobbits? You love Sméagol," he said. "There's no way you're gonna fall asleep."

"Hah! I've passed out so many times watching this," I said. "Even when I went to see it in the theater."

Stu chuckled. The next time he looked at me, I was snoring softly. He kissed my forehead and closed his eyes.

The next few days went by in a sort of haze. I wanted nothing more than to watch Becca and Bobby, but with Stu on day shift, it wasn't going to happen. Stu's request that I follow while he was working would be honored. I made it a point to text him asking if day-time stalking was out of the question.

No. Not at all. Just give me a heads up, was his response.

A wicked grin spread across my face. I'd figure out a day or two over the next few weeks to take off while Stu was patrolling the daylit streets. It didn't matter much if I were at the office, unless I'd scheduled a meeting or something. Barb was more than capable of running the place with me gone.

One night, Stu and I sat down with a calendar and my work planner. We looked at the weeks he would be on days and then cross-referenced the days

I didn't have meetings or other important things to get done in the office. When we sorted those out, we were left with over a dozen days to choose from. We agreed on a few loose days, largely because police work was never predictable. Ever. There was no such thing as "routine."

Having some sort of plan always made me feel better about anything. Stu followed our night of planning with asking about the body dump.

"In the Gulf," I answered.

"The same way you got rid of Andrew?"

"Yep. But the Gulf of Mexico," I shrugged. "So different."

"If you say so," Stu said.

"The fishes and Gulf Stream are fickle things," I said and left it at that.

Fifteen

TWO WEEKS LATER, I was able to take the day from work and follow Becca.

Stu was working and could go almost anywhere inside city limits, including the area Becca lived, even though she lived just north of the city line. If a call were put out on me, he'd say he was backing up the sheriff's department.

Becca started her day at home. I got the feeling she'd bore me to tears, more than Shae ever had. And that girl was fucking boring. She sat home and drank all night. It made her so easy to kidnap.

Three hours went by before Becca came outside. She was wearing jeans and a nice blouse. She got into her minivan, blonde hair blowing in the wind. I rolled my eyes at how perfect she always seemed. Pity I knew the truth. That she was a liar of the worst kind. Treacherous bitch.

And that snooty, Nazi stereotype-looking douchebag she called a husband. He had to be behind why she quit working for me; why she betrayed our friendship.

Sure, they'd been married when Becca and I became friends. Which is precisely why I felt he had too much to do with her treachery. He'd made no secret of the fact that he wasn't a fan of me. And I'd made no secret of my distrust of him. It was mutual. I'd never trusted him. But I did trust Becca. Big fucking mistake. One I'd be sure not to make again. At least I'd get to correct this one.

Becca pulled into the shopping center at Dale Mabry and Van Dyke. She got out and went into the HomeGoods store. We used to shop there often. Together. I sat in my Jeep and fumed while I waited hours for her to come out.

Then she went to Target. Today was decidedly the worst day I could have chosen to follow her. Not only was she dull and boring, but I wanted to shop too. And I couldn't because I was too busy trying to find a hole in her behavior to exploit.

Then it happened. She got out of her van and didn't lock it. It was too perfect, too easy. The van would enable me to transport both her and Bobby's unconscious bodies to the shop where I'd make them watch me cut their beloved open before killing them both and leaving them as sea life delight.

The day felt like a waste of energy. What it was was a huge waste of gas. Sure, it was better to be out of the office on a Tuesday, but still. I had been painfully bored and hot inside my Jeep all day.

By the time I got home, Stu was already there. He'd even made dinner. I walked in and was overwhelmed by the smell of spices and beef. I found something simmering on the stove and Stu out on the patio, grilling.

I kissed him on the cheek. "How was your day?"

"Good. Yours?"

I groaned and rolled my eyes.

"That good? Well, this dinner will make you feel much better," he cheerfully told me.

"What is it? I saw the pot on the stove—"

"Shit!" Stu exclaimed as he jogged into the kitchen and stirred the pot. "It's all a surprise. Go change. Relax. I've got this."

I stood there staring at him dubiously. He matched my stare.

"Fine," I huffed.

When I came back downstairs from changing—and taking some extra time to stare at my kill knife—Stu had the table set. I walked back into the kitchen, and Stu motioned for me to sit. Rather than try to help, I did as I was bade. There was a small plate with salad in front of me. In the center was a serving plate with a couple steaks on it. Next to that was a bowl of—what was that? Gravy? Stu's setting looked just like mine. He poured us red wine and sat.

I motioned to the bowl. Before I could get the question out, Stu answered it.

"My own special sauce," he said.

I giggled like a twelve-year-old, then poured some on my salad. It was delicious. Almost like the brown-bottled sauces, but less Worcestershire-y. There was even grated parmesan in it, giving it that creamy saltiness only parm could give. It was surprisingly delicious.

Stu smiled and dug in to his plate. We ate in silence for a few minutes; I was too busy enjoying Stu's cooking to say anything until I was about halfway done my steak. Even then, it wasn't much.

"Mmm," I moaned. "That sauce was amazing. Teach me your ways?"

Stu chuckled. "Maybe."

I smirked and stood, picking up the dishes and rinsing them before placing them in the dishwasher. Stu finished his dinner and brought me what was left on the table. I started the dishwasher and hugged him.

"Seriously, that sauce was the best I've ever had. Better than most steak places," I told him.

Stu blushed. "Thanks. I was just messing around one night and came up with it. It's nothing." He shrugged.

We capped the night off watching movies and drinking Earl Grey tea before going to bed. It made up for the rest of the day being a bust.

• • • • • • • • • •

I'd grown bored enough that I'd decided to waste another day following Becca. But on the way to her house, I changed my mind, opting to follow Bobby instead. Knowing his workday would be more beneficial than watching her shop and annoying me enough to kill her out of boredom. I killed people for reasons. And just about all of those people I'd had a connection with, I'd known them in previous times.

Bobby was backing out of the driveway by the time I arrived on their street. I only noticed because I had gotten too close to the house while looking for a good spot to wait.

A devilish grin crossed my face and I followed behind him about three car lengths behind. When he made a turn, so did I. There was traffic, making it all too easy to follow and not be noticed. Bobby was smart but not all that bright. That could have been my instinct speaking. I made a habit of checking to see if I was being followed. And it served me at least once.

I followed him all the way to his office in Lutz by the I-75 interchange. There I sat watching and waiting for about four hours. Then it was lunch-time. Bobby came out, hopped in his Honda, and left.

I watched him pull out of the lot and onto the road that would take him to Bruce B. Downs. The light turned red simultaneously as I pulled out of my spot. There were five cars between me and Bobby.

Soon we were on I-75 South, then I-275 into the city. He exited toward downtown and onto Pierce, as though he was headed to the waterfront. I followed him into a lot near the arena. He still hadn't noticed he was being followed, and I'd practically been directly behind him from the exit. How foolish.

I waited for him to pay and walk toward Channelside before hopping out and doing the same. Before truly walking away, however, I changed into sneakers. There was no fucking way I was walking around in heels. That would have been hell. I knew because I'd done it before. The blisters had been enough to sideline me from doing much of anything other than healing and soaking my feet. Fuck that. Not again.

I followed him to the waterfront and finally to the history center. Bobby shook someone's hand outside and was introduced to three more people. I hid by the corner of the building watching as they all exchanged greetings, shook hands, and went inside. As I started walking toward the restaurant, they came out to sit on the patio of the nearby Columbia Restaurant.

Trying not to be too much of a creeper, I chose a seat at the bar that allowed me to keep an eye on Bobby. I didn't need to be here. I could have just waited in my Jeep. But I was hungry and also wanted some unsweetened tea. Wine would have been ideal, but I still had to drive. I ordered a Cuban sandwich and sipped my tea, still watching the group. There was nothing even remotely interesting happening, just a lunch between colleagues. So I stopped paying that much attention.

I'd just finished my lunch when the group stood and shook hands again. That was my signal to pay the bill and get back to the lot. I did just that and got back before Bobby. He got into his Honda, and we made the uneventful drive back to Lutz.

He got off at the Fletcher Avenue exit this time. It didn't confuse me so much as it amused me. He still had no clue that he was being followed. Even when we pulled into his driveway and walked into his house, he had no idea that I sat a few houses away. Watching and waiting. I had nothing but time. Even if I lacked the patience to be calm about it.

I was fiddling with the steering wheel when Bobby came out of the house and waved in my direction.

Shit.

Sixteen

A CAR CAME UP on my left side and pulled up to the curb in front of Bobby. The driver's door opened and a woman exited. She hugged Bobby and they went inside. I breathed relief and took my leave. This person was an unknown and might be more perceptive than either Bobby or Becca was.

Stu was there when I got home. It was early afternoon, and he'd had the day off. He wasn't the least bit surprised to see me. He was, however, perturbed.

"Where were you?" he asked, his tone revealing indignance.

"I'm sure you already know," I answered, setting my purse and keys on the table inside the door.

"I do…"

I arched an eyebrow, waiting for the talking-to about Stu not being at work when I'd stalked. But it didn't come.

"I just want you to be careful," he said reluctantly.

"I know. And I am. I've been doing this a long time, babe."

"That's what concerns me."

I scoffed. "What? Why?"

"Because complacency happens. Even to the best of us."

I sighed. He was right. Well, half-right.

"I get that I really do. But you need to understand that the one thing I haven't fucked up yet is the stalking."

"Yet," Stu emphasized.

"Oh, fuck you. My natural sense of paranoia hasn't steered me wrong. I generally know when I'm being followed or watched."

"Except when you don't."

"That was a year ago! I've gotten better since then! What the fuck? I thought you were on my side." My voice rose and fell as I angrily defended myself. I was getting pissed off.

"It's not about sides, Brit. It's about keeping you safe and out of jail."

I huffed and grumbled unintelligibly and crossed my arms like a petulant child. Stu smirked at me as he came over to hug me. I shoved him away and continued to pout as I walked upstairs to change. My mood didn't change by the time I came back down. I flopped on the couch and stared at the paused show on the TV screen.

Stu sat next to me. "I'm sorry. I wasn't trying to upset you."

"I know. But you did. I'll get over it," I stated flatly.

Stu kissed my cheek and pressed the play button. He was watching something about unsolved cases. I watched with him until I couldn't anymore. Then I picked up the book on the coffee table and went out to the patio to read.

Before I realized it, I was finished with my book and it was dinner time. Stu slid the door open and poked his head out.

"Hungry?"

"Yes. Any ideas?"

"I've been craving tacos lately," he said, smacking his lips.

I nodded, excited. "Yes! From where?"

"That place in St. Pete on Roosevelt."

That settled it. We knew we'd get stuck in some traffic on the way there, too, but they made some of the most amazing chorizo tacos I'd ever tasted. Once that place was brought up, there was no way I wasn't going.

We hopped into Stu's car and took off. There were multiple backups on the 275, like always at this time, but those only made us hungrier. At one point, I'd mentioned I'd eat my own arm if we didn't get there soon.

And then we parked in the lot. I jumped out, straightening myself as I did. My stomach was making a lot of noise, more than it had in a long time. I shrugged and hooked my arm in Stu's as we walked to the restaurant.

The hostess asked where we wanted to sit. We agreed that outside was preferred, so she sat us there. She disappeared and reappeared with chips and salsa. I loved their salsa. It was always fresh and had a tang to it that most places' homemade salsas didn't. Then again, most people didn't like spicy food the way I did.

Soon we were clinking beer mugs and chomping on tacos. Mine were the soft kind and Stu's were not. We shared bites, though Stu stayed away from the refried beans and rice I had with mine. He'd even given me his, knowing I'd likely have them boxed to take home.

A dozen tacos and four beers later, we were full and happy. When I asked for the box, Stu chuckled heartily. I grinned, though I was too full to have a proper giggle without feeling wobbly. We settled the bill and tipped well before heading home. There was an accident at the bottleneck on the other side of the bridge—something that could always be counted on.

It was almost ten when we walked in the door. We were both still feeling the effects of being stuffed, but I waddled up the stairs to shower anyway. Stu fed the cat and followed behind.

Even though we'd had a bit of a disagreement earlier, the day had been an overall good one. I learned that Bobby really is as douchey as I'd initially thought, too. Okay, I didn't. I wanted to, but today wasn't that day. I hoped that the next time I followed him, I would find out.

And that I did. Again I'd chosen Bobby over Becca. Admittedly, I wanted to know if he was the jerk I thought he was. It was something that nagged at me. Maybe I wanted just to know I was right.

Bobby had left that day with a dirty grin on his face. It was the kind of dirty grin that said he was planning some shady shit. Or that he really was a douche. I was banking on douche. It would give me more reason to kill him too. Not that I needed the justification, but more of a release for me if the piece of shit I was killing had earned my wrath for more than one reason. I enjoyed it more if they deserved it more.

He started his day like he had the last time I followed. I sat outside in my Jeep for hours while he worked in his office. Again he came out at lunch. That was where the similarities stopped.

We drove down Bruce B. Downs and back to Bobby's house. Becca's minivan wasn't there. Bobby parked and went inside. I parked three houses down on the opposite side of the street. I wasn't in the ideal spot to be watching from, but it would suffice.

Twenty minutes later, Becca pulled up. She stopped at the end of the driveway and was waving her hands as though she was yelling at someone. Bobby came out of the house waving at Becca, and moved his car out of the driveway for her. When she exited the minivan, I could hear her screaming at him. I sniggered at the bougie nature of it all.

Bobby hugged Becca and kissed her. She seemed to be okay with that as an apology and they jogged in the house like two teenagers excited that Mom was out of town for the weekend. And then I was bored again. And disappointed.

Until I heard glass shatter.

Seventeen

BOBBY RAN FROM THE house. He was half-naked. I burst into laughter as a blonde woman who was not Becca chased him. They were followed by Becca. By the time the other woman was able to hide behind a car on the same side of the street as me, there were tears streaming down my face. Bobby was the douche I'd always dreamed he'd be.

Becca tossed the woman's clothes into the middle of the street. Bobby was calling after Becca as she stormed back into the house.

"Babe! I brought her over for us to *all* have a good time," he whined as the storm door slammed closed.

I laughed harder. Becca was too much of a prude for all that. Then again, I'd sort of thought the same about Bobby. But I also wouldn't have put it past him. Not that it mattered. He was still a slimy douchebag. He also came off as a bully. A bully that Becca listened to, for the most part. And it didn't seem that it was out of fear that she listened. Back then, it seemed that it was because she loved him. Gross.

The woman dressed herself quickly and got into a silver two-door car. She started it up and took off. I wiped tears from my eyes and face. Bobby was still outside in his boxers, pleading for Becca to let him back in the house. I wondered if any of the neighbors were recording video.

Finally, Becca came to the door and let Bobby in. They hugged and kissed and went back inside. I chuckled a little more before pulling out of my spot and heading home. The work-day was almost at an end anyway. And there was obviously nothing more for me to see. At least, nothing I wanted to see.

Back at home, Stu was gone. He'd be back in an hour or so. He had day shift again this week, which was one neither of us truly enjoyed. I preferred him to be on nights for obvious reasons. He preferred to be on afternoons because he wasn't getting home as the sun rose.

I started making dinner—crusty garlic-parm chicken breast with roasted carrot fries—while I waited for Stu to come home. It wasn't a normal thing for me to do, but it was a nice thing for me to do. There was still plenty of wine, too. So I opened a bottle of merlot and set the table. As I was pouring the wine, Stu came in.

"Smells good," he called from the front door. "Do I have time to take a quick shower?"

"Yep," I called back. "I just put it in the oven a few minutes ago."

I heard him take off up the stairs and the water start in the shower. I fed the cat so she'd leave us alone while we ate. I felt like a terrible pet mom for thinking about her that way, but she'd gotten incredibly jealous lately and had started sleeping on the couch in protest. I petted her while she ate and sipped my wine.

Stu came back down in sweats. It didn't matter what he wore he was still sexy. A year ago, I'd never have put that word in the same sentence as Stu's name. He was the furthest from that word back then. At least, to me.

I handed him a glass of wine and we toasted.

"To us," I said.

Stu smiled. "To us."

We clinked and sipped. Stu set his back on the table and looked at me as if I were trying to butter him up.

"What?" I asked, feigning ignorance.

He shook his head while chuckling. "Uh-huh. What are you up to?"

I batted my eyelashes. "Me? Nothing. I'm innocent."

We both giggled.

"I'm just glad you don't think that bringing home some random woman for us to share"—I made air quotes—"is a good idea."

Stu guffawed. "I'm sorry, what?"

I snickered. "That's what Bobby told Becca, any-way. Whether or not it's true...I think it's not. But it doesn't matter. He's a douche."

"I have to agree. Even if he did do it for them to share, if it was without Becca's agreement..."

I snickered again as I picked up my glass and sipped. Stu just shook his head. Then the timer on the oven sounded.

"Dinner's done," I stated happily.

Stu danced around the kitchen, trying to find something to help with.

"Anything I can do?" he asked.

"Yeah. You can sit down," I said, removing the trays from the oven and walking to ward the table. I placed chicken on each plate and dumped the carrots in the bowl in the center of the table.

Stu's face lit with joy. "It looks and smells delicious."

"Thanks. It's hot, too," I joked.

Stu was cutting into his by the time I sat down. I helped myself to some carrots and handed the tongs to Stu, who was blowing on a piece of chicken. The steam wafted to my face.

"Don't—"

"Ah! Hot, hot, hot," Stu said, exhaling on the piece in a pathetic attempt to cool it off.

I chuckled. He glared at me.

"Not my fault. I told you it was hot." I cut my own chicken and ate some carrots while it cooled.

When we finished, Stu patted his stomach.

"That was really good. Where'd you get the recipe?"

"If I told you, you wouldn't believe me."

Stu eyed me suspiciously but let it go. We cleared off the table, loaded and ran the dishwasher, and talked about our days while finishing the bottle of wine.

I told Stu about wanting to follow Becca but choosing Bobby instead. And of how boring the two of their lives—separately and together—are. They rivaled the dullness of Shae's alcoholic nights. At least she'd been amusing when we were out.

Stu told me about Officer Smith and her closing Andrew's case because there was nothing else to find. Even his parents had told her to close it out, that he would turn up sooner or later, likely in another state. That made me smile.

Eighteen

I DIDN'T REMEMBER HOW long ago I'd called my friend about needing more ketamine, but it finally showed up on my doorstep one Saturday afternoon. Stu and I had come home from a day on the Riverwalk to find it waiting for me. I nearly danced with joy. Then I remembered I was still outside. I picked up the box and carried it in as Stu opened the door.

Once inside and the door closed, I danced. With the box.

Chuckling, Stu shook his head and walked into the kitchen. I kept dancing my way up the stairs.

When I got to my bedroom, I opened the closet door then punched in the unlock code. I pulled the door open and my eyes sparkled. This light glimmered and glinted off the metals and shelves inside. Those things reflected in my eyes, along with the joy of seeing everything inside. My heart almost skipped when I saw my knife.

I plucked the case from the shelf and opened it. The light didn't reflect; the Cerakote prevented the reflection. Battleship Grey and black coatings stopped all of that. There was a slight—quarter-inch—bit of steel that wasn't coated. That was the slicing part. A friend had a machete that looked the same…Well, hers was all black, but the idea was the same.

I plopped onto the floor, legs crossed, and held it in my hands. My head dropped a bit as I took it in. Nothing else in that safe mattered as much as this knife did. It was as though it was more my child than Minion was. An inanimate object, it didn't breathe like she did, not like a child. But that didn't seem to matter. It was my child anyway.

Many minutes passed. I stared at that knife and it seemed to stare back at me. Not to see inside what soul I had left, but just taking me in as a whole. And I continued to stare right back at it. Though I took in whatever kind of soul it had, too. I watched and waited and absorbed. It had ideas and feelings all its own.

A noise on the stairs startled me, pulling me from my thoughts and feeling what the knife felt.

"You okay?" Stu asked.

I nodded. "Yes," I answered, my voice sounding small and far away.

"What's in the box?"

I heard the question but didn't answer. I was still feeling the knife's feelings.

"What's in the box?" Stu repeated, louder this time.

"Ketamine," I said nonchalantly.

"Ketamine? Isn't that what—"

"How I knock people out? Yes. Makes them easier to kidnap but heavy since they're passed out."

Without thinking, I picked the box up off the floor and pulled each vial out, one by one, and placed them on the shelf. The light gleamed off of them individually and as a group. It was a beautiful sight.

"That's almost blinding," Stu said.

I smiled, proud of the things I had accomplished—and still would. "It is," I said, still staring at the glimmers.

Stu stood behind me, not saying a word. We both simply took in the sight of the inside of the safe. I fingered my knife mindlessly, caressing the blade and its tip, the handle…

Stu put a hand on my shoulder. "I'll be downstairs. But hurry up please. I'm hungry." And then he was gone.

I didn't keep track of time while I stayed there. I just watched and took it all in, still caressing the knife. It was now and forever a part of me. I would feel everything it would feel. Including the last remnants of life draining from someone else. I'd already felt that, but now…now it would be more poignant. More visceral. Mine and mine alone.

Stu called up the stairs. I didn't understand the words; I was too lost in the sight in front of me. He called again, louder.

"Brit! I'm gonna eat without you!" he yelled.

"Hold your fucking horses!" I called back at him.

"Whoa…"

"Closing up now. Damn," I grumbled.

I closed the door slowly, so I could still admire the beauty within. I heard the door latch click closed, followed by the locking mechanism engaging. Knowing everything was secure, I went back downstairs.

Stu was waiting at the bottom of the stairs for me and shaking his head.

"You're in love with what's inside," he said before kissing me on the cheek. "What do you want to eat?"

I shrugged and walked to the kitchen. "I don't know. But I do know it's not already in this house."

"Figured that," he said. "I didn't find anything I'm in the mood for either."

"Chinese it is, then," I said pulling a beer from the fridge and twisting the cap off as I handed it to Stu. There was already a bottle of wine on the counter. It sat next to a glass. I poured some and tipped it to Stu. He nodded and pulled out his phone.

Forty minutes later, we were sitting on the couch eating and watching a newer superhero show. The food was good; the show was better. Chinese had always been my fallback when I couldn't decide what to eat and I was on the verge of being "hangry."

We watched three episodes of that show, then three more. That six hours caused us to not climb into bed until after 1 a.m.

Nineteen

THE SUN HID BEHIND a sheet of rain. The sheet of rain hid behind blankets of clouds. The humidity had nowhere to go; it nearly suffocated me as I jogged.

Stu was still at work, having moved from the swing shift for midnights. He'd be home around the time I'd be leaving for the office. So I jogged alone.

In my mind, I saw the inside of my safe. The picture flashed. Then I saw Becca laughing. It was foggy; only she was clear at first. Then I heard another laugh. It wasn't a joyous laugh; it was dirty and malicious. The picture grew clearer. Bobby stood next to Becca. They were both laughing maliciously; they knew they'd succeeded in lying to me. In betraying me.

I growled so loud, I heard people gasp over my earbuds as I jogged by them. Some even instinctively jumped back. One fell over the concrete rail that protected such people from falling into the bay. A giggle escaped, and I had to slow to a brisk walk so I could still breathe.

When I got my breath back, I picked the pace back up. Soon I was back home and in the shower, getting ready for a day full of emails and phone calls. My ears hurt just thinking about it.

By lunch, my ears were red and sore. I'd spent the majority of the morning talking to clients, new and old, and setting up meetings. It was usually Barb's job to schedule the initial meetings for new clients, but I'd decided to take that on myself so she could handle the data entry bits I hated. We had a good relationship that way.

As I walked through my front door, Stu sat up on the couch. Lines were embedded in his face where the pillows had been. I burst into giggle fits at the sight. Stu rubbed his eyes and glared at me.

"What's so funny?"

I took my shoes off and put them in their home by the door. I was still giggling, but I'd managed to breathe enough to speak.

"Your face," I said, running my fingers down my face in the shapes that littered his. "Lines…" I giggled again.

Stu stood, his face twisting in indignant frustration. "I do not look old—" he started.

I burst into hysterical laughter and tried to get him to follow me to the guest bathroom. Walking in front of him, I made beckoning motions with my hands and arms. He gave me dirty looks and hesitated. But he followed reluctantly.

Once in the bathroom, I flipped the light switch. Stu looked in the mirror and shock crossed his face. I giggled again.

"You're fucked up," Stu said a smirk starting to turn the corner of his mouth.

I grinned and kissed his cheek. Then I took off toward the stairs. I changed and came back down. By then, Stu was in the kitchen pouring a glass of water.

"Dinner?" he asked.

"I don't know. What I do know is that I need a ladies' night soon," I responded, pouring my own glass of water.

"It *has* been a while since you had one," Stu stated.

"I know." I sipped my water absentmindedly. The next time I tipped the glass back, nothing fell into my mouth. I'd emptied it and not realized it.

Stu came over and held me. "You okay?"

"I guess. I just...I don't know."

And I really didn't know. At that moment, all I knew was that I was exhausted. And angry. Bobby and Becca mocked me every time I closed my eyes. I felt like I was losing it. Maybe I was.

Stu kissed my cheek.

I came back to reality and looked into his eyes.

"You won't betray me, will you?" I asked.

He looked hurt. But his face quickly softened.

"Never. You go down I go with you," he said.

I dropped my forehead onto his shoulder and closed my eyes again. Becca and Bobby didn't taunt me for the time being. Instead, my mind's eye showed me a happy couple—Stu and me. Again, he brought me back to reality. This time slower, running his fingers through my hair. I looked up at him and smiled.

"I think I'm gonna go take a bubble bath."

"Sound like a good idea. I'll figure out dinner."

I shook my head. "I'm not hungry. Do whatever you want." I turned and walked upstairs.

I had no candles, but I did have a book to read. So I started the water, added bubbles, and stepped into the warm water. I relaxed as much as my mind and body would allow. And I read until the water cooled. I drained the water and got out, noticing that I'd gotten so lost in the fantasy world, I read half of the book. I smiled knowing Brian would be proud. I'd gotten somewhat back to the old days of allowing a book to truly draw me inside.

When I got back to the living room, Stu had a plate set out for me. On it was a plastic container. It was still warm. I opened it and found one of my favorite platters from the pancake place. I laid my eyes on French toast, scrambled eggs, bacon, and sausage. He truly loved me. And somehow knew my stomach better than I did. The smell was as heavenly as it had ever been.

Without a word, I grabbed a fork and dug in. Stu sat there, happily watching me. I'd finished it all in a few minutes. Then looked at him, suddenly feeling a bit embarrassed.

"What?" I asked, my face flushing.

"Why are you all red? You have nothing to be ashamed of," he said.

I shrugged. "I inhaled it. I don't think you've ever seen me do that before…"

"But I have," he said, smiling.

I kissed his cheek, noticing he didn't have any food in front of him. I paused a second too long, and he read my mind.

"I ate while you were getting dressed."

"So you inhaled, too?"

Stu nodded. I smirked.

"Guess no one can believe us if we say we never inhaled," I joked with a raised brow.

Stu chuckled.

• • • ● • ● • • •

Days later, I was still angry. I was still being mocked by visions of Becca and Bobby. To blow off some steam, I decided to head down to the garage in Ybor. I needed to make sure it hadn't been taken over or otherwise inhabited. That place was the best for killing people.

When I arrived, the street was busier than usual, but no vehicles were parked in the driveway. I drove by a few times just to make sure. When I was satisfied, I backed into the driveway on the side. It wasn't really much of a driveway, more like a wide sidewalk, but enough with semantics. I shifted to park, and got out, locking the Jeep on my way to the bay door.

The lock was still on this door. I smiled and kept walking. First around the back, then the other side. Finally, in front, I checked the lock on that bay door. Still intact. I wrapped my hand around the doorknob of the person door and turned.

Not good.

Twenty

IT OPENED, AND I about fell in, having not expected the door to be unlocked. At least I'd had pepper spray on me, if not a gun, and I held it at my side as I walked around. There was no one. Not in the office, not in the garage, not in the bathroom. I breathed a sigh of relief. On the way out, I noticed why the door had opened at all. The deadbolt was rusted and broken. I could replace the lock cylinder and no one would know. No one would be suspicious of a shiny new housing because I'd reuse the current one.

Added to the list of things I still needed to pick up: duct tape, rope, and now a new lock. I got into my Jeep and headed straight to the closest big box home improvement store. I knew they'd have everything I needed and didn't want to take chances on one of the mom-and-pop places not having something.

I was in and out in less than ten minutes once I'd gone inside. I was proud of myself for that. It had been the fastest trip ever into one of those stores.

I headed back home, my new supplies in the bag in the back. All but one roll of tape and the rope would stay in that bag. The rest would go into the safe.

Stu was home when I got there. He was back on the night shift. For that, I was grateful. I knew that if I decided to stalk Becca and Bobby tonight, he'd be around as much as he could be. At the very least, he'd be keeping an ear on his radio in case someone called on me.

There were still a few hours of daylight left. We decided to go enjoy it by the lake, feeding the ducks.

First, I had to run to the safe and put some things away. Stu smirked at me as I turned to go up. Then he was behind me, admiring the beauty and organization inside.

He held my face in his hands when I turned to him. The light reflected off the shiny surfaces inside the safe and into his eyes. They glimmered like the gems they were. He kissed me.

When he pulled away, his face was still wearing an expression of love.

"I didn't know it was possible to love someone this much." He smiled so big, I swore it would swallow those beautiful eyes.

I returned his smile and kissed him. Then we stood there holding each other for what felt like an eternity. The sun changed positions, and I noticed it before it really started to set.

"Still wanna feed the ducks?" I asked.

"Yes. Let's go," he said, taking my hand.

I pushed the safe door closed and we grabbed some bird seed before heading out.

The sun set not long after we got to the lake. Luckily, there were some lights nearby enough that we could still see. The ducks left us alone just before the mosquitoes came out. I slapped my arms twice before getting annoyed and beginning to stomp off. Stu chuckled at me the whole walk back.

"I'm going to change and head out," Stu said as we walked through the garage door.

I sighed. "If you must."

"Somebody has to try to stop the bad guy." He winked and walked away.

On my way into the kitchen, I chuckled to myself. *The bad guy*, I thought. *I love the way he thinks about me.* I knew he meant no harm, that I wasn't really the bad guy. I was more like the good guy. I *had* done the women of today's society a favor by killing Andrew. And those rude, twatty sisters. And Brody, the guy with the grossest gym etiquette ever…or lack thereof. Shae was more of a me kill. Alex was a half-and-half between me and society.

And those back in high school and college? They had been all for me, too.

I poked around the fridge and pantry, but nothing tickled my fancy. Sure, I had pasta and half of the things I needed for a decent salad. But I didn't want any of that. I wanted fast food. Something delicious yet gross. McDonald's it would be.

Stu came back down wearing his uniform pants and a white undershirt. The sleeves hugged his muscular arms, and I could see the ripples of his stomach. I never imagined that the man I met a year ago would look this good in such a short amount of time. But he'd pulled it off.

"Okay, I'm out of here," he said picking his duffle up from the bottom of the stairs. "If you go out…"

I nodded. "I'll let you know." I smiled and kissed him. "Be safe."

"I will. Love you."

"Love you too," I said and closed the door behind him.

Then I went into the garage and hopped into my Jeep. Greasy fries and a Double Quarter Pounder with cheese were calling my name. The drive-thru lane was busy; it was just after five and a lot of people stopped there on their way home from work.

Impatiently, I waited for my order. When the kid finally handed it through the window, he almost dropped it.

"Sorry! I'm…sorry!"

"It didn't fall. It's okay," I told him.

You're lucky it didn't fall, kid. I'd stalk you just to scare the shit out of you.

I drove home as quickly as possible, munching on stupid hot fries. I burned my mouth repeatedly, though I didn't seem to care. I didn't want them getting cold. The burger could get cold and still be good. The fries, however…

Minion greeted me at the door with her pathetic scream.

"You can have a fry when they cool down more," I told her.

I plopped down onto the couch only to remember that I hadn't yet given her food. So I did that and came back to my own food. I was halfway through my burger when she came back begging for the fry I'd promised her. They were cool enough, so I broke one into bits and set them down for her.

My phone chimed. It was the group text.

Next ladies' night? Danielle asked.

I don't know, but soon would be good, Kristen responded.

YES, Julie sent.

Tomorrow? I asked.

Three times, "yes" came back. But Sarah had yet to respond. So I called her.

She didn't answer. I didn't have to leave a voicemail, but I did. Even knowing that she'd see the text conversation and respond to that.

I finished my dinner and relaxed on the couch, reading the remaining chapters of my book. I'd still had a few left to be fully caught up on the series. But I needed to order them; I didn't have them waiting for me in the house. After I put the book on the shelf, I placed that order.

Then I'd gone up to bed and plugged my phone charger in. As soon as I walked away, it rang. I spun to answer it, hoping it was Sarah.

"Hello?" I answered, not paying attention to the caller ID on the screen.

"Aunt Brit?"

Twenty-One

WHY WAS BRIAN CALLING so late? And from whose phone?

"Brian? What's wrong?"

"Nothing. I swear. I'm fine, really."

"It's late, Bri. Are you sure?"

"Yeah. I just wanted to know how much further in the series you were. We're overdue for a discussion."

This wasn't right.

"Brian," I started, clearing my throat, "it's ten o'clock at night. Are you really calling me to ask about a book series? And you never answered whose phone you're calling me from. What's going on?"

He sighed heavily. "It's Julie's phone. Didn't you recognize the number?"

"No. Back to you. Talk."

"School wasn't that great today..."

I didn't say anything. Whatever was going on was something I couldn't pry into; of that I was certain. Beyond that, however, I didn't really know what had gone on. Had he gotten into a fistfight? Did someone hurt him? I waited for him to finish.

"Do you know anything about killing people?"

I tried not to choke on my own tongue. What was he getting at?

"I'm sorry? I don't follow."

"One of the other kids was talking about serial killers…I've never really seen or read anything about them. I was hoping you might have…"

"What about serial killers is so important that you ask me at 10 p.m.? And how have you not 'really' read anything about them? *Everyone* is curious about serial killers."

Again he was silent. I was growing impatient.

"Brian, talk to me. Now."

"I'm a lot like them, aren't I?"

I sat upright, covered in sweat. My eyes were open wide; I felt them.

It was all a dream. How long had I been asleep? I was in my pajamas and under the covers. What the fuck was going on?

Pulling the covers off, I noticed Stu in bed next to me. I shook my head, thinking that seeing him was also a dream. But it wasn't; he was there for real. I stood and disrobed as I walked to the bathroom. I went straight for the shower, tossing my pajamas into the laundry bin as I walked.

Why did I have that dream? Was I still thinking that Brian had a dark side? I must have. Right? Why else would I dream that he thought he was a killer?

I washed off and got out. I went to bed naked, afraid the dream would come back.

Stu woke me a few hours later. I was groggy and annoyed and borderline pissed off.

"Never mind, babe. You look like you barely slept. Go back to sleep," he said.

I rolled to my side and did just that for another hour. When I opened my eyes again, I heard the shower running. A tiny smile crossed my lips, and I rolled out of bed, thinking to join him. I wasn't able to sneak in; he was facing my direction and soaping up.

He smiled at me as I walked in.

"Morning, sleepy-head."

"Hi," I said, climbing in.

We switched places so I could wash my hair and face. The floor was slippery, covered in soap. I almost fell trying to switch back, but Stu caught me. I felt like today was going to be a long day.

And I was right. It may have been a weekend day, but my mind wouldn't shut up about the dream I had last night. Why was I dreaming that Brian was a serial killer? The kid was guilty of nothing more than lashing out at a teacher. He'd been in therapy since. And doing well. What the actual fuck was going on with my brain? I couldn't talk to Ben Peterson about it He wasn't just my therapist. He was Brian's, too.

I'd be able to figure this out on my own. Well, with Stu's help. I could tell him anything. I knew that. He'd be the one to help me. There had to be a reason for that dream. And I didn't think it had anything to actually do with Brian.

Stu had gotten out of the shower before me and made coffee before coming back up to finish getting ready for the day. I was putting on fresh clothes when he told me that he'd done that.

"Thanks, babe," I said. My voice sounded like it was echoing my brain. It was far away.

"What's wrong?"

"We can talk about it over coffee," I said.

Stu shrugged and walked into the bathroom. I went downstairs.

In the kitchen, the coffee pot popped and crackled, more than half-brewed. Minion sat on one of the chairs at the table, eying me like I was a shitty mother.

"Judgy girl, stop that," I told her as I pulled her food from the cabinet. She happily jumped off the chair and trotted to her bowl as I poured her food. By the time I put the container away, the coffee pot had stopped making its brewing noises.

I pulled two mugs down and filled one, leaving room for a few ice cubes. I needed the caffeine and had no desire to burn my lips or mouth. Stu came in as I took my first sip. I poured his mug and brought it to the table with me.

He nodded his thanks as I slid it across the table. He sipped then looked at me, surveying my face.

"So?" he asked.

I sipped and watched his eyes. I knew I could tell him anything, yet I was hesitating. I didn't know how to say it.

"I don't know how to say this, so I'm just gonna let it out. I had a dream last night that Brian called at like ten o'clock at night asking about serial killers. Then he asked something about him being like them."

Stu pondered that and drank his coffee silently. I tried to read his face as I drank mine. I was unsuccessful. Not that Stu was a mystery to me. Just that I couldn't figure out what was going through his mind.

He set his mug on the table and looked at me. I set mine down.

He took my hand.

"I don't think it means anything about Brian. I think it's your subconscious paranoia about yourself getting caught," he said thoughtfully.

I cocked my head to the side a little, absorbing what he just said. Then I squeezed his hand. He was right. Since Sweet's break-in, I was scared that someone else would think the same thing. But that they'd take it much further than Sweet had.

My thoughts were interrupted by a ringing cell phone.

Twenty-Two

I JOGGED UPSTAIRS TO retrieve my phone. As I picked it up, I disconnected the cord just in time to miss the call. It was from Sarah.

Unlocking the screen, it chimed again.

I'm game. What time? she asked the group.

Kristen and I expressed no preference. Danielle and Julie went back and forth, finally settling on 7 p.m. Sarah agreed to that time, too. That was it then.

When I got back to the kitchen, Stu was pouring us both more coffee. I filled him in on my plans.

"It's about time," he said with a chuckle.

I agreed and clinked mugs. Stu chuckled again. We sat in silence for a while, enjoying each other's company and our coffee. Words weren't always needed.

The doorbell rang, and I snort-growled like I did when annoyed or frustrated. Stu grinned at me stupidly. Had he never heard me make that noise?

I stood and plodded to the door. I felt like I knew who would be on the other side.

Opening the door with a painted-on smile, I wasn't surprised when I saw her fake smile.

"Hi, Britney. How are you?"

"We don't need pleasantries. What do you want?" I growled at the old lady from across the street.

She cleared her throat and stood straighter, if that was possible. "I wanted to apologize."

"For…?" I asked.

"Being such an old coot," she replied.

I was caught off-guard, of course, but I also wasn't entirely sure what she meant. My face revealed my confusion.

She cleared her throat. "I'm sorry. I've been a bitch to you. The president, VP, and a few others of the HOA brought it to my attention. I'd like to start over, if you're all right with that." She bowed her head.

I stood there, mind blown, thinking about it.

"Do you mind if I…" I thought better of that line and stopped, changing course. "Apology accepted," I said, fingers crossed behind my back. I didn't trust this olive branch, but I took it anyway.

I was still annoyed that the secretary of the board thought she could simply call owners out at whim. And for seemingly no real reason at all. What right did she have? And why was I defending this old bitch all of a sudden?

"Good," she said. "I'd really like for us to work together."

There was a moment of silence. Not out of honor. More out of discomfort.

"How?" I asked.

"At first, I thought you were nothing but trouble. Then I realized that you're a good person. But the men you attract…"

She shrugged.

I nodded, understanding what she was getting at.

"I do, don't I?" I giggled. "Weirdos, all. Well, except Stu. He's pretty normal."

She grinned in agreement. I could tell she thought he was cute.

The silence was awkward. I cleared my throat. "Soo—"

"—Now we agree to point out anything unusual," the old lady said.

I nodded. "Is that it?"

"Yes," she answered.

"Then you've got yourself a deal," I replied, extending a hand.

She shook it. "Good." Then she left.

I stood there, partially amused, partially annoyed. Stu called to me from the kitchen.

"You okay?"

I watched her walk home. "Yeah. Yeah, I'm okay."

He wrapped his arms around me and kissed my neck. "Clearly, she's not."

I smirked.

"She's not that bad," I said.

But she was. A real stick in the mud.

Stu pushed the door closed, his hand holding mine. I kissed him. He knew what was going on; I didn't have to elaborate. That old bat could spell my end. But neither one of us would allow that.

"I can't…"

"I know," Stu answered. "Too many people know about the animosity."

I nodded. My hands were tied. In more ways than one.

Weeks later, Stu was working while I was stalking Becca. Today she wasn't just out shopping. She was at the office. And meeting clients.

This was why I was always making sure I spent more than three days stalking. Mostly, she was dull and boring. Then there were the times she met with clients or friends. That was when changes in routine mattered most for me. For my purposes. Anything that could be viewed as unpredictable could also mean bad news where I was concerned.

So far, though, nothing was really unpredictable about the day. Becca had met the lady at Becca's office. Nothing unusual about that. They went to lunch down the road. Again, normal. Came back to the office…I wanted to pull my hair out. Becca was borderline unbearably dull; painfully dull. Instead, I waited and watched.

Finally, the women came out of the office building and shook hands. I rolled my eyes at the monotony of it all. Then, Becca surprised me. She'd first gone back into the building, which was what made me roll my eyes in the first place. But she came back out, looking around as if she knew she were being watched. But not by me. What the fuck? She'd looked all around, but never anywhere near me. Did she think Bobby was watching her?

Of course, I followed her. That was the only logical answer. I mean, she had no idea what I was, let alone where I was. I was sure she *thought* she knew. But she didn't. She'd screwed me over so bad. And I was the type to hold a grudge. And Becca deserved to die. Betraying cunt.

She left the lot, headed south on Bruce B. Downs. That alone wasn't strange; she lived in that direction. She passed Bearss. Again not strange. In fact, nothing about where she drove to and parked was strange. Until she got out of her minivan and into a white Kia Optima. It was tinted out, so I couldn't see inside; I had no clue who was driving. Becca got in the passenger side and the car backed out. I mentally noted the time before continuing to follow her.

The sedan got onto I-275 South, getting off onto I-4. Either they were headed downtown or east. I couldn't be sure until I saw the car bolt into the right lane, cutting off a semi-truck. The exit, however, revealed that they were, at the very least, going to Ybor. They could have been going downtown, too, but I'd only know if—

There it was. The turn for downtown. Just like that, the car parked in the convention center garage. The two exited the vehicle. The driver of the sedan was a woman. One I'd never seen before. Or had I?

As the woman placed her sunglasses over her eyes, I caught a glimpse. It was the same woman Becca had met and had lunch with earlier. But why were they being so secretive? Who was she? That would all be revealed in time, I supposed. But then it got weirder.

On foot, they walked across the bridge to Channelside Bay Plaza. The only things there really were restaurants. High-priced ones at that. But the view…The view was so beautiful. And distracting. It made it more difficult for me to concentrate. All I wanted at that moment was to stop and gawk at the skyline.

I shook my head and got back to business. Bobby held the door open for Becca and the woman. He watched them walk in, eying the woman's ass. I groaned in disgust and annoyance. How Becca to settle for the typical man. Gross.

Then it hit me what was going on. The three of them participated in extra-curricular activities. Together. Willingly. I felt my face turn green and lurched. But I stayed where I was. Waiting for them to leave. And then they did. The woman who drove the Kia was stumbling. Becca was laughing. Bobby held the door open again, appearing to be the perfect gentleman for two drunk and/or buzzed women. I knew better. Fucking controlling douche.

He let the women get back into the Kia, but handed the keys to Becca. She suddenly appeared sober. Their friend still looked too buzzed to dive. Becca got in behind the wheel, the woman in the passenger side. Bobby tapped the car and walked to his Honda.

I grinned, knowing what they were doing.

Twenty-Three

OR *DID* I KNOW what they were doing? In my mind, Becca and Bobby had gotten a woman drunk in an attempt to take advantage of her. In reality? In reality, I had no idea if she was consenting or not. I had only one way to know.

So I followed both vehicles back to Becca and Bobby's house. No matter that they didn't stop to pick up Becca's minivan. They could always do that later. All three adults walked into the house, the two women giggling. Becca still appeared the sober of the two, but not entirely sober. Regardless, it all seemed so…normal. Normal for them, not me.

Not much time had passed before I heard the screams. They were screams of pleasure and joy. The kind that only emanate when naked games were being played. I sniggered, thinking that it was just my luck to have to wait this nonsense out. What choice did I have, though? This whole escapade was abnormal. Not that it wasn't anything I hadn't had to suffer through before, but with these two…

Hours later, the three emerged from the house. They all wore grins and their faces were flushed. Clothing was thrown on haphazardly, but they didn't appear to care. The group was happy. The girls got into the woman's Kia, and Bobby got into his Honda. I let them get three houses down before pulling out of the spot I was waiting in to follow them.

Nothing eventful happened. They took Becca back to her minivan. Then she and Bobby drove home. Why Bobby had even gone in his car was beyond my comprehension. It was a waste of energy. Then again, not much that Becca did made sense. I still didn't know exactly why she did what she did. What I did know was that what she told me about why she left me and Osten was a lie.

That got me thinking about Osten. We'd agreed to get together more, yet neither of us had started to make good on that agreement. I pressed the button on my steering wheel for the Bluetooth and told my Jeep to call him.

"Britney!" he answered. "I was just thinking about you. How are you?"

"I'm good. You?"

"Wonderful!"

"Good to hear. Now, about our agreement to see each other more…"

He chuckled. "Yes, about that…"

We talked the rest of the drive back home. Plans were made for a few weekday lunches. One dinner was firmed up; another wore a question mark because I couldn't remember Stu's schedule.

"Well," Joe said, "get back to me after you talk to him. We've got time."

"Only if you stop ignoring what the cardiologist said about certain foods." I couldn't resist the jab.

Joe was a good sport about it, though, and chuckled. "I love you, too."

"Good. Chat soon," I said and hung up as I turned onto my street. Stu's Charger was in the street next to the driveway. I smirked, knowing he'd be proud that no one had called on me.

However, when I walked inside, my mirth quickly turned to surprise. Stu sat at the kitchen table. That much I could see. But then I heard a woman's voice. My face screwed up in a cocktail of anger and confusion. It clicked when I was halfway into the kitchen.

Stu looked up and saw me adjusting my expression to one that was somewhat happier than if I'd just eaten a lemon.

"Hi," I said walking in and kissing Stu on the cheek. I smiled as I turned my face to our guest. My face hurt from being this fake.

"Hello, Britney. How are you?" the old bat from across the street asked.

"I'm well, thanks. What can I do for you?"

"Oh, nothing. Stu and I were just chatting about how to keep the neighborhood safe." She sipped tea from the mug that sat on the table in front of her.

I fought back a growl. "Keep it safe from…"

"Hoodlums, of course," she finished. I nodded. Only old-school people used that word these days. I shook my head and chuckled bitterly.

"Right," I said. "Well, if you don't mind, I need to start getting dinner ready." I turned to the fridge and wrapped my hand around the door handle. "Excuse me."

She stood and spoke directly to Stu. "Thank you for the tea and the conversation."

"Least I can do," he said as he stood and escorted her to the door. He glanced back at me and made a face that exaggerated how annoyed he was that she showed up.

I acted busy, but in truth, I was. Preparing chicken to throw on the grill and pulling out things for a salad.

Stu came back in groaning. He plucked the mug from the table and brought it over to the sink.

"She practically forced her way in here," he grumbled.

"And you let a little old lady bully you," I said with a smirk.

"Just like you, I have to play nice. She blathered on about the news and the"—he made air quotes—"the rising crime rates." He shook his head, then walked to the fridge and pulled out a beer. He drew a long swig and thought for a moment.

"Because I, the friendly neighborhood cop, wouldn't know that what she's on about is fucking bullshit." He drank more then set the bottle on the counter. He wrapped his arms around me and kissed my neck. "How was your day?"

"Oh, you know, finding out my targets are into threesomes," I said jovially.

Stu spun me around. "They're what? Seriously?" He burst into giggle fits. "They seemed so uptight when I met them."

"Even when Becca and I were friends, I didn't know about this. So weird." I covered the chicken and let it rest on the counter. "No matter. I'm thinking to end all of their activities. Soon."

Stu eyed the chicken. "How soon? And when do you want me to grill that?"

He'd read my mind about dinner. Damn, he was good.

"It needs to rest about thirty minutes, so any time after that. And maybe a week or two from now…What do you think? Oh! And I've got one dinner with Joe planned, and we need to know your schedule to plan another." I'd thrown so much at him in forty seconds, I was surprised to see a smile cross his face. "What?"

"You," he said simply. "You're cute when you have a line of discombobulated thoughts that come out."

I didn't know how to respond, so I started cutting the lettuce for salad.

"When were you thinking to schedule the other dinner for? I can always switch shifts; I just need like a week's notice. And can you text me the date of the scheduled dinner? Or write it down? Not that I'll forget, but I will be helping you plan the—what do you call it? KSD?—so I may not be all up on our commitments. I'm still learing how to balance these things."

"KKD. And yes, I'll write it down for you. And text it. Can't be too reminded, right?" I slapped his butt.

"Careful," Stu warned, "we may not have dinner when you want it."

We both snorted.

While we waited for the chicken to absorb the flavors it rested in, Stu put the news on for the weather. There wasn't yet a video of just that portion; it was too early. The seven-day was back to typical Florida at this time of year: warm and semi-humid in the mornings, but warm nonetheless. It would be good body-dump weather. We grinned at each other once we realized that.

I sighed when I realized something else.

"What's up?" Stu asked.

"Boat," I mumbled.

He nodded. "Maybe we should look into buying one?" he suggested.

"Maybe. I'd thought about it before, but didn't think it would be needed. Now, though…" I sighed again.

Stu put his hand on my shoulder in an attempt to console me but stood suddenly. I looked up at him, somewhat annoyed.

"Nothing to say?"

"I want to get the grill warmed up. I'm starving. But I also really have to pee," he said as he trotted to the guest room.

I giggled. I pulled the same shit occasionally. Then I stood and headed to the kitchen to finish getting dinner ready. Stu came through and right out onto the patio to start the grill. I did what was needed for the chicken and pulled the salad from the fridge.

By the time we'd finished dinner, Stu was ready to pass out. So was I. Neither of us cared that it wasn't even 9 p.m.

Twenty-Four

OVER THE NEXT FEW days, Stu and I continued our conversation about buying a boat. It seemed the most logical thing if that was how I planned to continue disposing of bodies. And it was. Sure, the pigs were a good way, too. And I could still use them if I chose to. Maybe I would, but if we were to buy a boat…Well, that would be a hefty investment.

Stu's voice broke me from my thoughts.

"I could always captain it and maybe charge for small parties to fish," he said.

"You could, but that would take away from our time off together," I replied thoughtfully.

We talked on and off for a few more hours. The agreement was that we'd rent another boat this time and go from there. We'd take more time to plan the next kill so we could research more about even buying a boat at all. I liked the Bayliner Stu had rented a few months ago and wouldn't have minded one of those. But it felt like such a waste of money since we wouldn't use it for much else than body dumps.

We were on our way to Joe's for dinner. The current topic was changed as we drove closer. I held a bottle of whiskey in my lap. It was a gift for Joe. A client had recommended it to me, so I meant to share it with those who would appreciate it more than I would. Stu and Joe were fans of sipping whiskey.

Marsha greeted us at the door when we rang. She wrapped her arms around me like I was her long-lost sister.

"It's really good to see you, Marsha," I said hugging her back.

"You too, Britney! I made apple pie," she said.

I smiled.

"More for you than the boys," she said smiling and taking my hand.

"What about me? Where's my hug?" Stu complained after we'd gotten three or four steps inside. Marsha turned and hugged him.

Stu laughed. "You really didn't have to. I was just kidding."

"I know, but I did feel kind of rude," Marsha said.

I giggled as she came back, took my hand, and dragged me into the kitchen.

Stu peeled off at the living room; Joe was sitting in a chair facing the hallway. He'd waved to Stu, and Stu took that as his grand escape. Silly boys. I was glad that they'd be able to enjoy the whiskey without us ladies gabbing to ruin it.

While they enjoyed their whiskey in peace, we sipped some pinot noir and caught up. My mind kept wandering, though. And I felt a jolt of anticipation every time I caught myself imagining stabbing Bobby as Becca watched. That was the ultimate high: watching someone you used to love watch their beloved suffer.

I was far away when Marsha snapped her fingers in my face.

"Sorry, what were you saying?"

"Where have you been? You've been in and out of this conversation since we sat down," she said.

"The water," I half lied.

Her face screwed up in confusion. "The water?"

"Yeah. Stu and I have been talking about maybe buying a boat. But we wouldn't be out on it often enough to justify the cost," I said.

"I'd come out on it. I love the calm of the ocean," Marsha said.

I perked up a bit. Boat parties could be fun. But would they be enough for us to buy one? I'd have to run it by Stu to see what he thought about it. And that's exactly what I told Marsha.

We'd drunk half the bottle by the time dinner was ready. We grinned at each other, each of us knowing that the other may or may not have been buzzed. I helped Marsha serve the food, if for no other reason than to be helpful and observe her more.

Marsha ushered me to sit, then ran into the kitchen for one last thing—another bottle of wine. When she came back, she poured some into my glass then hers. The men were still sipping whiskey and water.

Dinner was amazing, as it always was when Marsha cooked. Tonight's menu was cast iron cooked top sirloin. It was heated to perfection; mine was the best medium-rare I'd ever had. I swore it almost mooed pitifully at me. There was also mashed potatoes from scratch, cornbread, and butter. For dessert, the aforementioned apple pie made specifically for me.

The three of us complimented Marsha on her excellent culinary skills like we always did. This time was different, for me at least. Something about our deepening connection screamed at me. I couldn't yet translate my feelings into words, though. I filed it away in my brain to analyze later. Tonight was about good food with good people.

We talked for a few hours more, until Stu looked at his watch and practically fell out of his chair in shock.

"It's almost midnight," he said, "I should get this girl home before she turns into a mouse."

"Hah!" I scoffed. "So I'm a horse, am I?"

We all got a good laugh at that. Especially me. It had been a long time since I last saw that movie where mice were transformed into horses by the fairy godmother. As in I was a child.

And just like that, Stu and I were on the way home. Chatting again about the possibility of a boat. I'd hugged Joe and Marsha goodbye, with Joe and I knowing we had lunch plans again soon. Marsha winked at me and grinned. I'd winked back.

Then Stu and I were in bed after I rinsed the day off my skin. We lay there—me staring at the ceiling—in silence.

I was sure I'd drifted off when I heard Stu's voice. It was a dream, right? I rolled over and opened my eyes, groggy from the little amount of actual sleep I'd gotten.

Simultaneously, I jumped and screamed, falling out of bed.

Stu was still watching me as I pulled myself back up.

"Such a fucking creep," I muttered, climbing back under the covers.

Stu smiled. "I-I just love you. Sometimes I think we're not real, that's all."

"And that gives you license to be a creep? Okay then." I rolled over and tried to fall back to sleep.

"Soon," Stu whispered in my ear.

I grinned wickedly and closed my eyes again.

Twenty-Five

FINALLY, THE DAY WAS upon us. Stu and I had gotten out of bed extra early to make sure we had the plans down.

I'd inject and drag Becca; Stu would have Bobby. We'd take them at the office. Taking them from outside their house would be too dangerous. So we dressed in touristy clothes and followed them to the office. They chose to drive Becca's minivan that day, making it that much more "normal." I cackled at the notion of that word.

I drove my Jeep, and Stu his Charger. We'd put our prey in our individual vehicles, making transport not only easier for us, but scarier for them if they happened to wake up. I had more ketamine with me, just in case.

We arrived at the shop in Ybor before 7 a.m. It was still somewhat dark out, covering our entrance to the garage. I pulled in first, followed by Stu. As he shifted into park and got out, I closed the bay door. These two had been stupid easy to knock out and throw in the back. At least Becca had been. What a lightweight. And then I scooped her over my shoulder.

Stu secured Bobby to the desk with plastic wrap, while I chained Becca to the lift post. I opened my bag on the hood of Stu's Charger, gingerly setting aside the things I'd need for the kills. As I did that, Becca woke up and screamed. I heard Stu talking in hushed tones to her. She squealed and squealed. I could only imagine the things he was telling her I'd do. I smiled at the thought. Once my kill knife was out, I slowly turned to face them. Becca screamed again.

Stu held his own knife to her throat. She stifled.

It was no use hiding the knife; Becca had seen it. So I kept it at my side in a less-than-threatening way.

She knew better. She sensed it. Even before Stu uttered a word.

Stu stepped back from her and went to stand by Bobby, watching Becca's face the whole time.

The next time Becca opened her eyes, my nose brushed against hers before I stepped back so she could see me. She screamed. I laughed. Stu smiled. Bobby groaned and stirred. Stu turned his attention there, and I focused on Becca.

"Tell me the truth," I said to her.

"I never lied to you!" The fear in her voice dripped like sarcasm from mine. I ate it up.

"But you did," I said running the tip of the knife down her cheek. I made it a point to start at her eye and work down ever so slowly, as if I was caressing her. She shuddered, nearly cutting herself open. I snickered.

"Careful," I cautioned. "Shudder any harder, and you'll definitely cut your face open."

Bobby chose that moment to wake up. Stu had him wrapped to the desk so well that Bobby could only do baby crunches to move around. The only free appendage was his head. It was like watching an octopus whose tentacles were being held together. I was greatly amused.

I shuffled over to Bobby. Becca screamed louder.

"No! Don't! Please!" she begged as I approached Bobby. "Take me instead!"

I spun on my heel. "I'll have you soon enough," I spat and turned back to Bobby. "First, you will suffer. I will kill him while you watch."

Becca screamed again. This time, Stu shoved a rag in her mouth. I didn't know where he'd gotten it from; it didn't come from my bag. But did that even matter?

Bobby looked at me, eyes wide. He tried to hide the fear in them, but it didn't work.

"Whatever you want, Britney, it's yours," he said trying to bargain.

I laughed. "You have nothing I want. Try again, shitbag."

"I have connections," he said, a single tear rolling down his face. He'd come to terms with the fact that no matter what he said, I'd still kill him. He knew that better than I did.

Again I scoffed.

"At least make it quick," he said.

"Not a chance," came my retort.

He made a motion that looked like a shrug. At least the guy knew he was a douchebag.

Becca continued to sob and beg for their lives, even if Bobby wouldn't. She knew it was futile, yet she continued.

I brought my knife up against her neck. She squealed again. I smiled. It was possible the devil was inside me then.

I brought the knife above my head and back down in a diagonal motion, slicing her forearms. She screamed in pain. I snickered. The adrenaline rushed in my veins. I sliced again. Again Becca screamed. Again and again, I sliced her arms and chest. She kept screaming.

Then Bobby spoke up. "Stop! Please, stop!"

I didn't bother speaking to him; neither did Stu. I slashed and slashed and sliced. Both Becca and Bobby screamed. Blood pooled on the desk under Bobby and dripped off onto…was that…it was! Stu had placed open contractor bags under the desk! My fuck, I loved this man. In that moment of excitement, I simultaneously brought the knife above my head and grasped it in both hands. I grinned at Becca, then slammed the knife into Bobby's chest.

"NOOOOOOO!" Becca wailed. "No! Bobby!" She erupted into sobs so hysterical she started hiccupping in seconds.

I circled the lift as Becca writhed and screamed and sobbed. When she calmed down—not out of want, out of exhaustion—she slumped over. I slid over and brought her attention back to reality with the tip of my knife under her eye.

Becca bolted upright and screamed.

"Hi," I said grinning into her face. "Please don't scream again. It's getting old."

She turned her head slightly to face me. I grinned again. She choked back a scream.

By that point, I was too annoyed, but I needed a real reason why she betrayed me.

"Why did you do it?" I asked. "Tell me and I'll let you go."

"I-I-I didn't like the way I was treated for being naturally pretty," she sputtered.

I cackled again and brought the knife down, piercing the skin on her chest. She screamed.

"Answer me!" I ordered.

"Okay, okay," she said. "Bobby wanted me to quit so we could work together at his firm," she said bursting into tears. "I didn't want to leave you. I wanted to tell you, but he made me—he made me lie!"

"Did he, though?" I asked her, my expression revealing nothing. My face was blank; I didn't believe her and she knew it.

"I'm sorry," she pled, "I'm so sorry, Brit. I love you."

"I loved you, too," I whispered in her ear as I brought the knife down and into her chest. In seconds she was gone. And I felt a weight lifted.

Stu kissed my neck hotly, but I brushed him away.

"We don't have much time," I said. The sun was slowly rising.

"You're right. I already bagged Bobby and threw him in the trunk," he said. I hugged him. He took my knife and wiped it off before stowing it in its case, and back in the bag. I really did have the perfect man for me.

Twenty-Six

WE TOOK THE CASH-RENTED boat out into the Gulf side of the Gulf Stream and dropped the cinder-block-weighted bodies in their cut-up bags to the bottom. I'd done the research. The bodies would be less than bones floating along with the current in a few days. I was satisfied and high.

So was Stu.

When we got home, we cleaned our tools and showered. Then we had the hottest sex of our relationship. We barely made it through another shower before passing out in bed.

• • • • • • • • • • •

We woke up on Thursday morning, with me thinking it was Saturday. I panicked for a little while, until Stu handed me my phone so I could see for myself. Then I chuckled and called Barb to tell her I wouldn't be in. And possibly not tomorrow either. Stu was already off the next two days, so no worries there. I rolled over to put my head on his chest, and we went back to sleep.

I opened my eyes to darkness. And a cat standing on my chest, screaming in my face.

"Sorry, kid," I said to her, rolling out of bed. I pulled my robe on and padded down to the kitchen to feed her. When she was happily chomping away, I started back up to my room. It was only 9 p.m., and I was still beat. Between the dual kill and the hot love-making with Stu, I could definitely go back to sleep until morning.

Which was just what I did.

• • • • • • • • • • •

Weeks later, we were grocery shopping when I locked in on my next reason.

Acknowledgments

This book, let alone series, wouldn't be possible without the following people and references:

Practical Homicide Investigation (5th Edition) by way of a Thomas Harris acknowledgement. The FBI's *Serial Murder Multi-Disciplinary Perspectives for Investigators* Report (available free online), and *psychologytoday.com* for helping me add the necessary depth to Britney.

Ret. Sgt. Chuck Burns for his consultation where the textbook didn't answer specific questions.

Justin D., for helping me on ridiculously short notice with some nicknames.

Nathan, for his advice and invitations. I'm so very grateful I finally decided to take you up.

Mark…sweet Mark. Without you, I wouldn't be here. I love you more than I can express and always will.

Jason, for the awesome editing and blurbs and feedback and advice and just being you. You have made me the writer I am today. Let's not get arrested, please. At least not before we make that money.

Also by Amanda Byrd

13 Reasons for Murder:
Politeness Kills (#1)
Meathead (#2)
Philistines (#3)
Hungry (#4)
Bad Blood (#5)
Betrayal (#6)
Disillusioned (#7)

The Morgan Davis Serials
The Girl at the Bottom of the Ocean (#1)
Before You Die (#2)

Anthologies
Thrill of the Hunt: Cabin Fever (Thrill of the Hunt Anthology Book 6)

The Dr. van Wolfe Saga
Trapped (book 1)
Moratorium (book 2)

Medicate (book 3)